The Field

Robert Seethaler was born in Vienna in 1966 and is the author of several novels including *A Whole Life* and *The Tobacconist*. *A Whole Life* was shortlisted for the Booker International, read on Radio 4, garnered huge acclaim and was a *Sunday Times* bestseller.

Also by Robert Seethaler

The Tobacconist
A Whole Life

'Melancholy, tender, comic' *Spectator*

'If the dead were to talk among themselves, what would they discuss? Life, of course. Robert Seethaler makes this response the heart of his new novel, *The Field* . . . each devoted to a person who has lived in the small town of Paulstadt since the end of the Second World War, Seethaler brings lives to life, revealing their secrets, hopes, regrets and joys. To the extent that the reader has the impression of looking at all these fates through a keyhole . . . There are premonitions. There are memories. Both can deceive. What is not deceptive, however, is the talent of Robert Seethaler.' *Le Monde*

'In the same way that the protagonist Andreas Egger from *A Whole Life* was a hero in the classical (i.e. literary, not biographical) sense, *The Field* takes into account an entire web of events, entire lives that would have been forgotten, were it not for Seethaler's imagination and writing craft. Seethaler's love of his characters touches the reader.' *Frankfurter Allgemeine Zeitung*

'The prose of Paulstadt's deceased is simple and sparsely beautiful. And in this sparseness lies the strength of the book and its author. Robert Seethaler is a master of nonheroic narration. And his calm, unflustered tone suits his new novel very well. In its best moments, his gentle, beautiful account of failure is reminiscent of that literary saint, Robert Walser.' *Die Zeit*

'The real topic: life stories, memories, reckonings and confessions, experiences, disappointments and certainties – beyond death. And to these, Seethaler applies his literary skill, which produces meaning through casual observation. Seethaler produces a wonderful, constantly unfolding novel – on life as it could be, or could have been, in Paulstadt or elsewhere.' *Spiegel*

'The literary craft of Seethaler's new novel is displayed in his ability to narrate heavy subject matter lightly. His language, which is simple without being simplified, makes the following clear: every life is minor and major at the same time and fraught with contr. . . . . ler's *The Field* is a b. . . . . m being a tear-jerk. . . . . ORF

Robert Seethaler

The Field

Translated from the German
by Charlotte Collins

PICADOR

First published 2021 by Picador

This edition published 2022 by Picador
an imprint of Pan Macmillan
The Smithson, 6 Briset Street, London ECIM 5NR
EU representative: Macmillan Publishers Ireland Ltd,
1st Floor, The Liffey Trust Centre,
117–126 Sheriff Street Upper, Dublin 1, DOI YC43
Associated companies throughout the world
www.panmacmillan.com

ISBN 978-1-5290-0807-4

Originally published in 2018 as *Das Feld* by Hanser Berlin
an imprint of Carl Hanser Verlag GmbH & Co. KG, Munich.

1 3 5 7 9 8 6 4 2

A CIP catalogue record for this book is available from the British Library.

Typeset by Palimpsest Book Production Ltd, Falkirk, Stirlingshire
Printed and bound by CPI Group (UK) Ltd, Croydon, CRO 4YY

Visit **www.picador.com** to read more about all our books
and to buy them. You will also find features, author interviews and
news of any author events, and you can sign up for e-newsletters
so that you're always first to hear about our new releases.

The Voices

The man looked out over the gravestones that lay before him as if strewn about the meadow. The grass was long and insects were buzzing in the air. On the crumbling cemetery wall, where elder bushes ran wild, a blackbird was singing. He couldn't see it. His eyes had been giving him trouble for some time now, and although it got worse every year, he refused to wear glasses. There were good reasons why he should, but he didn't want to hear them. If anyone said anything to him about it, he told them he'd got used to it and felt at ease in his increasingly blurred surroundings.

When the weather was good, he came every day. He would stroll around for a while among the graves before eventually sitting down on a wooden bench under a crooked birch tree. The bench didn't belong to him, but he thought of it as his bench. It was old and rotten; no one else would trust a bench like that. But he greeted it as if it were a person, stroking his hand over the wood and saying, 'Good morning,' or 'Cold night, wasn't it?'

This was the oldest part of the Paulstadt cemetery, which many people simply called 'the field'. This area had once been uncultivated land owned by a cattle farmer named Ferdinand Jonas. It was a useless patch of ground, littered with stones and poisonous buttercups, and the farmer had been happy to get rid of it at the first opportunity by selling it to the parish. It wasn't any use for grazing cattle, but it was good enough for the dead.

Hardly anyone came here any more. The last burial had taken place months earlier; the man had forgotten whose. He remembered another burial more clearly, many years ago, when the florist Gregorina Stavac was laid to rest on a rainy late summer's day. Gregorina had lain undiscovered in the storeroom of her flower shop for more than two weeks, dust collecting on the cut flowers as they withered on the shop floor. The man had stood at the grave with a handful of other mourners, listening first to the words of the priest, then only to the hissing of the rain. He had never exchanged more than a few words with the florist, but on one occasion, as he was paying, their hands had touched. After that, he had felt strangely connected to this unassuming woman, and as the cemetery gardeners started shovelling in the earth, his cheeks were wet with tears.

Almost every day he sat under the birch tree and allowed

his mind to wander. He thought about the dead. Many who lay here were people he had known personally, or had encountered at least once in his life. Most were ordinary citizens of Paulstadt: craftsmen, businessmen, workers in one of the shops on Marktstrasse or its little side streets. He tried to recall their faces, piecing his memories together to create images. He knew that these images did not conform to reality, that they might bear no resemblance at all to what these people were in life. But that didn't matter to him. It gave him pleasure to see the faces appear and disappear in his mind's eye, and sometimes he would laugh quietly to himself, leaning forwards, hands folded over his stomach, chin sunk on his chest. If anyone had been watching him from a distance at such a moment – one of the gardeners, perhaps, or a visitor to the graveyard, wandering down the wrong path – they might have had the impression that he was praying.

The truth is, he was convinced that he could hear the dead talking. He couldn't understand what they were saying, but he perceived their voices just as clearly as the twittering of the birds and the humming of the insects all around him. Sometimes he even fancied he could pick out individual words or scraps of sentences from the swarm of voices, but however hard he listened, he never managed to piece the fragments together so that they made sense.

He imagined what it would be like if each voice were to

have the chance to be heard once more. They would talk about life, of course. He thought that perhaps a person could only really pass judgement on their life once they had gone through death.

But perhaps the dead had no interest whatsoever in the things that lay behind them. Perhaps they would talk about what it was like over there. How it felt to stand on the other side. Summoned. Called home. Gathered in. Transformed.

Then he dismissed such thoughts. They seemed sentimental, almost ridiculous, and he began to suspect that the dead, just like the living, would utter nothing but trivialities. They would whinge and brag; they would make complaints and idealize memories. They would grumble, scold and cast aspersions. And, of course, they would talk about their illnesses. In fact, it was possible they would talk about nothing but their illnesses, their lingering sickness and death.

The man sat on the bench under the crooked birch tree until the sun went down behind the cemetery wall. He stretched out his arms as if measuring the patch of ground in front of him, then lowered them. He breathed in the air again. It smelled of damp earth and elderflower. Then he got up and left.

It was closing time on Marktstrasse, and the tradespeople were carrying the crates and stands of underwear, toys, soap, books and cheap tat back into their shops. Roller shutters were rattling down on all sides, and at the end of the street the greengrocer's cries rang out as he stood on a crate distributing the last of the melons.

The man walked slowly. He dreaded the thought of spending the evening sitting at the window looking down at the street. From time to time he raised his hand to return the greeting of someone he didn't recognize. People must have thought him a contented man, glad of every step on the sun-warmed pavement; yet he felt insecure and out of place on his own street.

He stopped in front of the plate-glass window of what used to be Buxter's butcher's, and leaned in towards his reflection. He would have liked to have seen himself as a young man. But the eyes gazing back at him no longer held any spark capable of igniting his imagination. His face was just old and grey and rather shapeless. At least there was a small bright-green leaf caught in his hair. He flicked it away and looked back. Margarete Lichtlein was walking along on the other side of the street, confused as ever, pulling her handcart full of the shopping she had never bought. He nodded to her and moved on. He walked faster now. A thought had come to him, or rather a notion, concerning time in his life. As a young man he had wanted to pass the time; later, he had wanted to stop it, and now, in his old age, he wished for nothing more fervently than to regain it.

This was the thought that occurred to the old man. He didn't yet know what he should do with it; in any case, he wanted to go home first of all, as it got chilly after sundown. He would go to his store cupboard and permit himself a little drink. Then he would put on his comfortable brown trousers and sit at the kitchen table, with his back to the window. In his opinion it was only like this, with one's back to the world, in peace and quiet and with no distractions, that a thought could be thought through to the end.

Hanna Heim

When I was dying, you sat beside me and held my hand. I couldn't sleep. I hadn't needed sleep for a long time. We talked. We told each other stories and reminisced. I looked at you, as I had always liked to look at you. You were not a beautiful man. Your nose was far too big, your eyelids drooped, and your skin was pale and blotchy. You were not a beautiful man, but you were my man.

Do you remember: I was new to the school, and on the very first day, in the staffroom, you asked me what was wrong with my hand. It's deformed, I said, nothing to be done. You took it and looked at it. Then you pointed out of the window and said: do you see that tree over there? Its boughs aren't deformed, they're just crooked, because they grow towards the sun. I thought that was a bit corny, to be honest. But I liked the way you stroked my fingers with your thumb. And I liked that incredibly big nose. I think I thought you were rather dishy.

Fifty years later, you were still holding my hand. It felt as if you had never let go, and I told you so. You laughed and said, it's true, I haven't!

I don't remember my last words. But they were addressed to you, of course; how could it be otherwise. I asked if you could open the window. I thought a bit of fresh air would do me good. And then? What did I say then?

What I do still clearly remember are the first words I said to you. It was before our conversation in the staffroom. That morning I arrived and saw you crossing the playground ahead of me. I stopped you and asked the way to the principal's office. Excuse me, I said, I'm new here, can you help me? I asked you, even though I knew the way. You just said: come with me, miss, and walked on ahead in silence. You walked with big, heavy strides, slightly bent forward, hands clasped behind your back, the way you always walked. The morning sun was shining and the striped shadow of the front gate spread in a wide fan across the asphalt. I was wearing a mint-green sheath dress with a white collar. The dress was a present from an aunt; I'd spent hours altering it to fit me. I'd cut the collar off one of my father's old shirts and sewn it on. My hope was that it lent me an air of assertiveness and confidence, but already, as I followed you across the playground, it seemed prim and old-fashioned and I felt ashamed.

Isn't it strange: I remember the colour of the dress I

was wearing all those years ago, but I can't remember what season it was when I died.

It never occurred to me that you might be a teacher. Part of me was still sitting in a classroom with satchel and pigtails, so to my mind all teachers had to be old. Old, grey women and men who smelled of coffee and chalk and whose authority had worn thin over the years, like the sleeves of their woollen cardigans. But you were young. You wore a creased shirt with an open collar and leather sandals. No one wore sandals back then. Perhaps I thought you were the father of a pupil, or the school caretaker, I don't remember now; not a teacher, at any rate. Or perhaps I wasn't thinking any of this as I followed you towards the school building; perhaps I was just contemplating your hands on your back. Your fingertips were so rosy, as if they were glowing, shining with a light all their own, all by themselves.

You opened the window. Your figure in silhouette. The curtain, billowing for a moment in the draught. The light. It must still have been day. Or had day come round again? When you got up to go to the window, you set my hand down. You didn't just let go, you placed it on the pillow beside my head, and I breathed my life's last breaths into my small, deformed hand.

You didn't like coffee. Coffee doesn't just blacken teeth but hearts as well, you said in the staffroom. Look around – black-hearted colleagues, every one of them, creatures of the devil! Some laughed. Most pretended they hadn't heard. Only Juchtinger, the old maths genius, took you at your word. He threw open the windows and let in the warm air. Enlighten us companions of the dark, he cried, blinking his inflamed eyes at the summer sun.

I lay in bed, listening to the muffled gurgle of the heating pipes in the wall. (So it was winter?) The pain that had clawed at me for so long was now just a faint memory I carried inside. A moment had come when suddenly it was gone, but I knew that this relief only signalled the beginning of the final farewell. There was still a little time, though. And you sat on the edge of the bed and held my hand. And we talked . . .

Come with me, miss! I didn't catch the irony in your words at first. This form of address seemed perfectly natural to me. I followed you as we walked across the latticed shadow on the asphalt. I could hear our footsteps; the echo bounced back off walls that were reddened by the sun. We walked in silence. Now it occurs to me, though: we did speak again, just before we plunged into the shadow of the entrance hall. Careful, you said. And I said: yes. But what were you warning me about?

Your shape at the window. The slightly slumped shoulders. Your narrow, narrow back. Behind it, even now, your clasped hands. How often have I seen you stand like that? From the day we moved into the apartment, you loved looking down at the street. Sometimes, coming back from afternoon classes or doing the shopping, I could already see you from afar, up there at the window. If I was carrying heavy shopping bags, I would put them down to wave to you. Weichselstrasse 11, second floor. Who would have thought that our first apartment together would also be our last?

We entered the school building, and suddenly you vanished. It must have been my blood pressure; I'd hardly slept the previous night, and I hadn't eaten anything that morning, and for a few moments I stood in lurching darkness. When I resurfaced, you were already on the big staircase. Without turning to look at me, you ran swiftly up it, two steps at a time. And I followed you. Our footsteps clattered and echoed in the cool silence.

You held my hand. You stroked your thumb across my fingers, across these bent twigs. Your other hand rested in your lap. When you talked, you closed your eyes. Your eyeballs darted about behind your eyelids, following the pictures. Daylight bathed your face. Then the light of the night. I often heard your watch ticking in your lap, and the days and nights went by as if they had shrunk to hours. Sometimes we would fall asleep together, and when we woke everything was as before.

You asked me where I'd come from, and I gave a silly answer. From outside, I said, where else? I think I thought I was being rather bold. Children's high-pitched shouts and cries could now be heard in the playground. The staffroom gave a collective sigh and began to move. Old Juchtinger closed first the window, then his eyes. Your thumb lay still. From outside: that's a a long way to come, miss, but you're here now!

You placed my hand on the pillow. The material felt smooth and cool. My warm breath. The creak of the floorboards under your feet. Your back, your shoulders framed by the open window. The light seemed to pulsate around you. I think I heard the clatter of a lawnmower. Or was it the snowplough? Did I tell you to close the window again? Did I talk about tomorrow? Did I tell you that I love you? Do you remember?

Gerd Ingerland

'In this world there are sheep and there are wolves, but you don't get to choose. You can't take your pick, you understand? It's not a decision, it's fate. But you're lucky: you're a wolf. You're strong, you've got staying power. You won't get devoured. You're a devourer. No one knows what wolf's meat tastes like. Fate is on your side. You're one of us.'

I was ten when Papa said this to me. He worked at the bank, and about twenty ties and a row of brushed and ironed suits hung in his wardrobe. 'Things are good as they are, and they're getting even better,' he used to say, sitting on the sofa and looking around the room. Mama, sitting next to him, would put her hand on his and nod. Her fingers would play with the long black hairs on the back of his hand. I never knew whether she liked those hairs or hated them. The way she tugged and plucked at them, it looked as if she was trying to pull them out.

My first memory also has to do with hair. I'm tiny, and

I'm sitting on the floor behind a curtain. Somewhere a window is open; the curtain is moving, sunlight shimmering through the cloth. Then it's pulled back and my mother is standing there, crying. Or perhaps she's laughing; in my memory it makes no difference. She lifts me up. Her hair smells of kitchen and Sunday morning. It's long and blonde and it feels as if it could cloak my whole body, as if I could disappear in Mama's hair.

Later we moved into an attic apartment behind Markt-strasse. The apartment was cramped, with a low ceiling, but I could watch the pigeons on the roofs around us. Sometimes a kestrel would appear, and bats reeled over the chimneys at dusk like small, drunken shadows.

I collected beetles, flies and other insects. I tried to catch them alive, then put them in a little metal tin. If you held the tin to your ear, you could listen to them dying. Then they slowly dried out and became as hard as pebbles.

Papa went to the bank, I went to school, and every morning before breakfast Mama would hang our clothes over the backs of our chairs: a fresh suit for him, a shirt and trousers for me. She would do this with a funny, lopsided smile. She did almost everything with this crooked smile on her face. I couldn't say exactly what it meant, but I had the idea that perhaps she was proud of us.

I got bigger, had friends, was interested in girls, and had no problems at school. Everything was as it should be. My understanding was that life was worth living. I didn't know where it would take me, but I was sure I was on the right path.

Then something happened. It was late summer; I had just turned seventeen. Three of us were crossing the school playground, a great expanse of asphalt with no shade. The cast-iron gate to the street loomed up in front of us. It was as tall as a house, black with gold tips that shone in the afternoon sun. High in the sky a flock of waxwings passed over, throwing a flickering shadow onto the yard. For a few moments the flock moved up and down like a veil in the wind before suddenly dropping and vanishing behind the school building. It was hot. The chewing gum of generations of schoolchildren had softened on the asphalt and stuck to your soles with every step.

Johannes Storm, a boy from the parallel class, was standing in the street. He wasn't that tall, but his shoulders were broad and strong, his ribcage like a barrel. He had a big, childlike head and short blond hair. His eyes were very close-set, and when he spoke to you he could barely look you in the face. No one had anything to do with him outside school. But everyone knew that he lived with his mother, a vulgar woman who scrubbed the pavement outside the shops on Marktstrasse and cleaned their plate-glass windows.

He stood smoking and staring at the ground as if there was something incredibly interesting to be found there. We lined up in front of him, and I said he should give me a cigarette. He didn't even shake his head. A string of tiny beads of sweat glistened at his temple. He held the cigarette in his left hand; the right was stuck in the pocket of his trousers. I said I didn't want any trouble, just a cigarette. He didn't reply. A lorry laden with rubble and bits of metal clattered past on the road. The driver's hand hung from the side window, fingers tapping on the bodywork in time to some inaudible music. The lorry turned into a side street and the clattering died away. Inside the school building some girls were shouting; then a window slammed shut and all was quiet.

'Didn't you want a cigarette, Gerd?' My friends were standing half a metre behind me. We were inseparable back then. A few years later I couldn't even recall their faces.

I stepped closer to Storm. 'I'm sure you don't want any trouble,' I said. 'Or do you? Do you want trouble, Storm?'

He didn't answer. He just stood there, staring at the ground, blowing out smoke. Then he dropped the cigarette butt and glanced up. He looked straight past us, towards the playground where a few small children were now running. I could feel the sweat trickling down the back of my neck. It felt as if the heat were penetrating every pore and filling me to the brim. I looked him in the eye and said, 'I'm going to devour you!'

It's crazy, but I really wanted to do it. I tried to grab him and pull him towards me, but before I caught hold of his collar he whipped his fist out of his trouser pocket and punched me in the stomach. I doubled up, but before I could slump to the ground he rammed my forehead with his knee and I stumbled back against the iron bars, then sank slowly down them onto the pavement. I saw their gold tips swaying high above like reeds in the wind. Storm's head appeared over me. I wanted to crawl away, but I didn't know where to, so I closed my eyes, curled into a ball and covered my face with my hands. I felt my ear throbbing on the ground, louder and louder, and for a moment it was as if I could feel the earth's pulse through the paving stones.

I completed my time at school, and on the whole I fulfilled expectations. When I walked out of the gate for the last time I didn't turn around but stared fixedly ahead. I wanted to believe that I was still on the right path.

At nineteen I left Paulstadt to study. It was a mild morning, and as the bus left town I laughed, but it was a weary laugh; I didn't trust it any more.

My plan was to complete my economics degree as quickly as possible and then embark on a successful career. I went to lectures, enrolled in seminars, and tried to take part in student life. We met every day in one of the many pubs scattered around the university. There was a lot of talking. It was usually about politics, and as alcohol was always involved, the discussions would get heated. I only drank in moderation. An indeterminate fear lurked in my heart, and sometimes, when things got too loud, or someone leaped up, their face twisted with aggression, I felt cold terror welling up inside. 'Stop it,' I would cry. 'Please, stop it!' But the others would just laugh, and I confined myself to sitting silently on the sidelines; if anyone looked at me, I would try to smile.

In the second year, I fell in love with a girl. She was very beautiful; at least, I thought so. Her skin was the colour of blossom honey and unmarred by a single blemish; not a speck, nothing. It was smoother and softer than anything I had ever seen or touched before. If I wasn't near her, I was sick with longing; but the day I went to her apartment, stood on the threshold and talked about the softness of her skin, she laughed so uproariously that I thought I could still hear her laughter echoing on the stairs long after I was back out on the street, trembling with shame and anger.

It felt as if my brittle heart had finally fallen to pieces. I stopped going to the student meetings and spent the evenings alone in my room. Weeks passed, each day just like the next, until someone slipped the news under the door in a pale yellow envelope.

Papa is dead.

You read the words and don't comprehend them. It's not pain and it's not sadness. It's just strange. Time seems to stand still around you, set in a kind of aspic around which your own thoughts buzz like flies grown sluggish in the autumn. And in the room next door the same song keeps playing on the radio, always the same one, over and over again.

Mama and I organized the funeral. It wasn't a farewell, it was just something to be dealt with. We didn't weep at the graveside. The bank sent a bit of money, and I moved back into my old room, where I found the tin of insects in a drawer. I didn't throw it away, but I didn't open it, either. I left things as they were and settled back into the little kingdom of my childhood.

With Papa's death, Mama had stopped smiling. The lopsided smile just seemed to have disintegrated. And with her smile her face disintegrated, too, and, later, all of her. My mother vanished almost imperceptibly, and it was only many years after her death that I realized I was alone.

I found work at the Lainsam & Sons insurance company, where I shared an office with three women. Our job was to sort the bills and check the balance sheets. One of the women, Sonja, was convinced she saw something in me, and one evening we went on a date. We drank wine, which was a mistake, because afterwards she wanted to come home with me. I brought her back and we sat on the sofa. I started saying whatever came into my head, and I almost didn't notice when she touched me for the first time. Later, she placed her cheek against my cheek and I breathed her in, dazed by the wine and the scent of her hair, and perhaps everything would have been different if I hadn't had a mishap. She said I shouldn't worry, it could happen to anyone. She stroked my head the way you stroke a little boy.

A few weeks after this episode, Sonja handed in her notice. She wanted to try a new beginning, she said, start a new life, and as I watched her clear her desk, scooping things from her desk to her handbag with an energetic sweep of her arm, I had a vague sense that she was taking my potential as a man along with them.

I was confused and hurt. Nonetheless, I also felt a kind of relief, and perhaps Sonja would soon have been no more than a blurred memory if I hadn't seen her on a street corner three weeks later, locked in a close embrace with Johannes Storm.

It had been raining since early morning, a cold, drizzly November rain; the foggy grey of approaching dusk had descended on the town, and the lights of the streetlamps and neon signs were trembling in the puddles. I was on my way home from the office, hurrying along Marktstrasse, where autumn leaves were drifting as if on a dark river, when I saw them. They were standing under the awning above the door of Sophie Breyer's tobacconist's. He was holding her with both arms; her head was resting on his chest. She had closed her eyes; he had raised his head slightly and was looking out at the rain. I hadn't seen him since school; he'd gone grey at the temples, but his face with its close-set eyes hardly seemed to have aged. His hand slid slowly down her back. A movement passed through his body, like a shiver. Then he turned his face in my direction, and I saw his nostrils flare.

That was all a long time ago. In my memory it never stopped raining; the world drowned. Now I lie here, between my parents. My path was not a long one. But it's peaceful here, and sometimes at night I hear a distant howling. Very soft at first, a high, even note, like a child crying; then it quickly swells, grows louder and more urgent, until it seems to fill the night. I lie still, listening to the howling of the wolves, until all of a sudden it breaks off. Then I know: it's just the wind blowing through the hole in the cemetery wall. Through the head-sized hole old Schwitters' degenerate son kicked in the wall, when he was wasted on beer.

Sonja Mayers

I used to visit my grandfather after school on Saturdays. We would sit at his table and play chess. Occasionally he would forget my name, or what the piece in his hand was called. Sometimes he would ask when his wife was coming home. Granny had been dead for twenty years, but I couldn't tell him that. I'd say: she'll be back late today. That would calm him, and we could play on. Her photo stood on the chest of drawers. A young woman, not especially pretty, nothing remarkable about her face. She was wearing a pale blouse and a necklace. Her smile was thin and gave nothing away, but Grandpa believed she was poking fun at him. Once I took the photo out of the frame to look at it more closely. There was something written in pencil on the back.

> 21/3/III.
> I became ill
> and died

the heroine
of my tragedy
entitled:
ALL IN VAIN

Grandpa didn't know what to make of it, either. I stuck the photo back in the frame and we went on playing. He thought for a long time, then said: I'm moving my soldier to C7.

Father Hoberg

I was three years old when the war ended, and five on the November day when Father came home.

He stood in the doorway, pale, a leather duffel bag over his shoulder, looking down on me from above. His heavy coat hung open over a jersey full of holes, and when he lifted me up and pressed my face against his chest I could feel the dampness of the wool. Mother was standing behind me, in the kitchen. Her ragged sobs were drowned out by the weather forecast on the radio.

The following Sunday we went to Mass. With my father holding one hand, my mother the other, I entered that lofty space for the first time. The tops of the chestnut trees in the churchyard were swaying behind the stained-glass windows, and the brightly coloured saints looked as if they were alive.

The wind blew in with us through the door, sending flickering waves through the flames on the rows of votive candles. Mother held her hands over them and told me to do the same.

We're warming our hands on people's wishes, she said.

The pews were packed. In their dark coats, fur hats on their bowed heads, the congregation looked like a herd of tired, heavy animals. Here and there a whisper was heard, a stifled cough, a creak in the wood.

Breath steamed.

When the organ began to play, I wanted to jump up and run outside. The sound filled the space right up to the cross vault. It seemed to have the power to burst the walls. Then I felt my mother's hand on my knee, and I stayed.

I started to sense the urge during the Kyrie, and by the end of the first reading I could hardly bear it.

I need to go, I said.

Not now, said Father.

I tried to hold it in. Doubled up, fists pressed into my lap, I sat between my parents' stiff coats, murmuring invocations. During the Gospel I started crying quietly, and during the cleansing of the Temple, I sat down again.

I need to go, I said.

Sit still, said Father.

So I opened my arms and let go. When the Son of man shall come in his glory, and all the holy angels with him, then shall he sit upon the throne of his glory, declared the priest at the front of the church as I wet my trousers and the tears ran down my face.

You'll wear those trousers until you go to bed. You are a disgrace to God the Father.

It was also on a Sunday, almost fourteen years later, that Father died of the lung disease he had struggled with ever since returning home. The end, when it came, was quick; there was no one to whom he needed to say goodbye, and before midday he was carried out of the house, as shrivelled and light as a bundle of dry brushwood.

A few weeks later, my mother followed him. Heading home with a full shopping basket on her arm, she suddenly stopped, tilted back her head, and seemed for a few moments to focus on a distant point in the cloudless sky before lurching to one side and falling down dead in the middle of the pavement. Four big red summer apples rolled out of the basket into the road where they lay for a while, shining in the sun, until, one after another, they were caught beneath the wheels of the rush-hour traffic.

After that, I was alone. I had only confused ideas about what the long remainder of life might consist of, and I went in search of answers. I talked to people I met, but they didn't speak to me. I stood for hours at my parents' grave, and they certainly didn't speak to me. I sat at the bar in the Golden Moon, but the schnapps and the dullness of my thoughts just made me feel sick. I got on the bus and travelled out across the fields to the terminus and back again. I leaned my forehead against the window and saw the passing landscape disappear behind my cloudy breath, but apart from that nothing happened.

One day I went into the church. I sat in the seat where I had let things take their course all those years ago. I remembered feeling safe between the bodies of my parents. My mother's warmth. My father, who was so big, yet only one of many. And I remembered that forbidden, uncontrollable urge, and my salvation, accompanied by shame and desire.

From then on I came every day, and eventually the priest noticed me. I'd always made sure I was alone; I usually came at midday, as not even the oldest, loneliest people strayed into the church at that time. So it was all the more of a shock when he was suddenly standing beside me. He was short, and in the soutane with the black cincture around his stomach his figure seemed delicate and feminine. I felt as if I'd been caught red-handed, and when I glanced up and looked into his face, the tears sprang to my eyes.

I have called thee by thy name; thou art mine.

Although it was this priest's affection that prepared the way for me, I don't remember his name. Nor do I remember ever having heard it. He once said that only offices and authorities were interested in names; before God we were all just *humankind.* That pleased me. I liked him a lot. And right after our first meeting, after he wrote the Word on my forehead with his thumb and I stepped out of the shadowy church into the bright sunlight, I decided that I would emulate him and choose the priesthood as my profession. My search was at an end. He had found me. Overcome with anticipation and joy, I laughed across at the construction workers sitting on their scaffolding on the other side of the street. They said nothing, just bit silently into their rolls. Beer sloshed in their bottles.

The seminary was a long way from home; I felt like an outsider there, and was considered odd. I had neither friends nor enemies. I wasn't interested in the others. Their aspirations and mine had nothing in common. While they played football or recited psalms in the evenings, I knelt in my room and prayed up against the wall until I saw the star-studded cloak of the *Mater ter admirabilis* in the cracks in the plaster.

I took a razorblade and carved three crosses into my chest out of sheer gratitude. I didn't tell anyone.

After graduating from the seminary, I stayed away from home a while longer, but then the priest died. He had recommended me as his successor, and so I came back to commence my service to the parish. People mistrusted me. They put their heads together and whispered. They smiled about me, this young, thin, peculiar man who stood outside the church door on Sundays and greeted every one of them with a handshake. But He had chosen me, and when I preached, He spoke through me. And His messages were not only those of joy and deliverance. There were also messages about the terrors of love, the travails of patience, and the sacrifice of devotion, and often I would stand at the altar, seized with burning zeal, crying: Your pain will pass, because you are in God, and God is in you!

There was a thought in me. An idea that had ignited in my heart, that carried me through the days and kept me awake at night. I wanted to show people the way. I wanted to purify and strengthen them, and I wanted them to follow me. And I knew – I knew! – that I would have the strength to do it.

One morning, in the summer of the year when no rain fell and the houses were grey with dust from the fields, I went to the church to cast myself before the altar. All night I had walked around town, wrestling with feelings that kept surging up within me, feelings of doubt and of the futility of all my endeavours. I had walked the silent streets beneath the moon with nothing in my ears but the echo of my own footsteps, and I had said to Him: My Father, stand by me, do not let me despair when confronted with gloom, guide my feet, strengthen my hands, quicken my spirit and drive the fear from my heart, guide me, my Father, that I may guide the people out of the thicket of ignorance and the thorns of falsehood along the path to the one true light.

So I walked through the night until day finally dawned and the town rose up out of the darkness. I saw the last creatures of the night stagger out of the Golden Moon and head in different directions. I saw the florist unload from her car the bouquets of fresh peonies, carnations and hyacinths that she had picked up at the wholesale market, and take them into her shop. And I saw two old women sitting on a bench, watching a pigeon peck up crumbs at their feet.

Behind the town hall a skinny boy was balancing on the kerb and pulling a dog along behind him. He kept yanking violently at the lead, and the dog whimpered, trying in vain to brace itself against the ground. Come on, said the boy, or I'll give you what for. He had a high, childish voice, trembling with tension and annoyance. The dog gave a brief, choked cough, then lay flat on its stomach and abandoned all resistance as the boy dragged it on through the gutter. I planted myself in his way. Stop, I said. The boy looked at me. He was angry, but I could see the fear and distress behind his anger. Don't be afraid, I said; all living things are equal before God, we are His creatures, we are all one in His lap.

The boy took a step back. I saw his eyes widen, and at that fear rose up in me, the hot, searing fear that he might not understand me, that he might turn away.

Stay there, I ordered him sharply. Purify your soul, confess before God the Almighty and beg Him for enlightenment!

He turned away, but I grabbed him by the shoulder. I was shaking. I raised my face to Heaven and cried: O Lord, take up this boy! Take him into Your lap! Take him into the protection of Your eternal love! Redeem him, O God!

As I shouted, I heard, as if at a great distance, the dog's whimpering and the boy's scream. A shudder ran through his body. He wrenched himself free and ran off.

For a while I stood motionless, gazing upwards. Four pigeons minced along the roof ridge of the town hall, one after another. The television antenna rose up into the sky like a spindly cross, glowing in the morning light.

When I lowered my eyes again, everything had changed. I had finally attained clarity and recognized the enormity. Yet instead of sinking into despair, I was filled with calm. I felt light and free; it wouldn't have taken much for me to burst out laughing in the middle of the street. An elderly couple were passing on the other side of the road. They were walking arm in arm, and the woman was speaking animatedly to her husband. They stopped and looked at me for a moment, then turned the corner and disappeared.

I entered the church. It was quiet and cool. Dust swirled in the dim beams of light. The saints stood frozen in stone. Between two pews, a hymnal lay open on the floor.

Dass Du mich einstimmen lässt in Deinen Jubel. That I may join in exalting Thee.

*

A single votive candle flickers on the stand. I take it and carry it up the aisle. I do not cross myself. I do not kneel. I do not listen to the voices.

I hold the light in my hand.

The white cloth is draped over the Table of the Lord, who is no longer at home here. I hold the flame to the corners and it immediately catches fire. A cool draught gusts through the church, and the flames leap up. The crucifix is first to ignite. Jesus crackles and snaps. As he breaks free of the cross and slowly topples forwards, he looks as if he is laughing. The altar burns. I walk behind it, with the candle, to the pile of hymnals. They catch as if soaked in petrol. I throw some of them high into the air. They flutter for a moment like burning birds before plunging into the pews. One of the books slips under the curtain of the prayer niche. The curtain billows, then ignites in a single, noiseless explosion. The flames roar and crash among the benches. Blisters unfurl in the wooden varnish like glowing flowers with threads of smoke rising from them. I am at peace, because now I know everything. The windows burst above my head and the saints scatter in a rain of colourful splinters. The wind blows through the window cavities, fanning the flames higher. The pulpit burns, light trembles in the water of the font, and high up, in the darkness under the roof, sparks whirl like dancing stars.

Nabil al-Bakri

On my gravestone it says: GOD IS GREAT AND WE ARE HIS CHILDREN. Who the hell carved that there, I wonder? I am the son of my mother, Ayesha al-Bakri, and my father, Abu Nabil Muhamed al-Bakri. Whether God also played a part in my genesis I can't say. I never got to know him.

I was nineteen when I arrived here with my parents, after a long journey. It was winter, and cold. The first time I saw snow on the streets I thought there had been an accident. Father wrung his hands. We want to create a garden of Eden in this desert of ice, he said.

He opened the shop on Marktstrasse, *Uncle Abu's Vegetables and Exotic Fruits*. Although he had long since turned a deaf ear to the unadulterated word of God and decided to go through life without any other creed, force of habit made him unroll a small rug in the cellar several times a day and send his prayers towards Mecca from among the potatoes and swedes. When one day the Turkish plumber, whom he had called in to repair a burst pipe, revealed to him that he'd got the direction wrong and had for years been turning his backside to the Kaaba instead of his face, my father thanked him and counted out twice the usual tip into his hand.

Not to worry, he said. After all, Mecca is everywhere.

The plumber nodded. Cabbages floated past their knees.

In the beginning I sorted plums, polished melons, or scrubbed the squashed fruit off the pavement. Later, I got my own apron and was allowed to serve customers. I liked the smells and colours. I loved to hear walnuts clicking in their sacks, and when no one was watching I would plunge my hands deep into the basket of lentils, or let almonds and pistachios trickle through my fingers. Mother and I stacked the peaches and nectarines into artistic pyramids, and I would drive out into the fields with Father to negotiate with the farmers.

The business did well over the years; we had all we needed. I can't say whether my parents were happy, but I saw them smile a lot. They didn't live to be very old, but their deaths were peaceful.

After my parents died, I took over the shop. I white-washed the salesroom, hung strings of colourful little lights around the window frames and ordered new aprons.

I painted over *Uncle Abu's Vegetables and Exotic Fruits* with ochre-yellow paint and nailed a big wooden sign above the entrance: *Nabil al-Bakri's Fresh Fruit and Vegetables – from all over the world.*

I gave a party to celebrate the reopening. There was music and sweet dried fruit all day long. Many more people came than I had hoped, and late that evening, when the last guests had left and I pulled down the rattling shutter, I knew it would all be all right. I sat down in the dark and placed my hands, palm upwards, on my knees. I had a strange impulse to thank God. I recited what I believed to be the right words. But even as they were coming out of my mouth, I thought about them, and the more I thought about them, the more meaningless they seemed. They were empty and brittle like the fruit crates stacked in the cellar.

I got up and stepped outside again. The evening was warm; it smelled like rain. The lamp came on at the street corner and moths fluttered in its light.

I understood the business. I knew everything there was to know about it, and in time I learned to understand the customers, too. You can learn a lot about people by watching them choose their fruit and vegetables. I noticed when they touched a peach with their fingertip, like a lover's skin. I saw how they bent over the crates to smell the lemons and nuts. How they wrapped a lettuce in newspaper, lovingly, like a baby in a blanket. I listened when they talked about their worries, their husbands, wives and children, their misfortunes and illnesses. And I didn't stop listening when they got annoyed about something, when they shouted, waved their arms and pointed their fingers, convinced they knew exactly what's what.

Sometimes Father Hoberg came by. He looked at the tomatoes in the sunlight, weighed the apricots in his hands, and eventually he started talking about God. I told him I was just a greengrocer and knew nothing about such matters. But the priest was stubborn. He asked me questions to which I had no answer. He irritated me, with his fervent voice and his restless hands that pounded on my wooden pallets. Torrents of words poured out of him, one after another, and then I got angry and started talking and shouting as well. I couldn't understand why God was supposed to be truth and truthfulness when his creation was so imperfect. Nor could I see any sense in the destruction of Sodom and Gomorrah, where neither women nor children were spared. This made no impression on the priest. God's mercy is infinite, he yelled. But by then I wasn't really listening any more, and I don't think he was hearing my words, either, and so we talked and shouted at the empty air until our strength failed us and we stood facing each other as if awakening from a delirium.

May His mercy drop also into your heart, said the priest, and give me two bunches of spring onions.

*

I stood in that shop for forty years. I loved the work and was never ill for more than a day. Over time, my weight wore a hollow in the floorboards at my post behind the scales, a little pit in which I felt secure. I never married, and I didn't long for children. I was seldom lonely, had no great desires and was sensible enough not to fulfil my dreams. I donated money towards the reconstruction of the church, and to the food bank at Christmas. I gave poor Margarete Lichtlein an orange every day after her son's accident. I asked my questions of people, not God. I listened to you all. I looked you all in the eyes. I forgave you when you sprayed the shopfront and smashed in the windows. When you called me camel-driver, I laughed and stuck a picture of a camel caravan on the door. I laughed whenever I liked. There were so many days when I left my sadness in the cellar. I honoured my parents, paid my taxes and scrubbed the pavement every evening. I took nothing with me and left nothing behind. I had only this one life.

Seven years before my death, I took my parents' ashes home. The Holy Book forbids cremation, but no one was very interested, and in any case, such prohibitions had lost their significance for my father. He didn't believe in Hell any more, only earthly existence, and his just happened to reach its end in Paulstadt. Before they were laid to rest, I removed a little scoop of ash from each urn so I could smuggle them out of the country in two small linen pouches, disguised as powdered spices.

I took the bus from the airport. The driver smiled at me in the rear-view mirror.

Are you from here? he asked.

I don't know, I said.

Mashallah, my friend.

Mashallah.

I got out at the village square. The brightness hurt my eyes. The bus shelter, behind which I used to play with stone marbles, had disappeared. Everything looked different. Only the great cypress was still there. My father had often talked about it. It was so old that the prophets had rested in its shade before setting off into the world. Its roots went so deep that the furthest tips were scorched by the heat of the Earth's core. That's why sometimes, at night, you can see its cones glowing in the moonlight.

I walked through the village streets, inhaling the smell of the old walls. I was hot in my shirt and dark trousers. The sweat ran down my face. There weren't many people about. A few children. A small group of elderly women, all in black.

Some men were sitting outside a café, drinking tea. I remembered the entrance, with its carved ornamentation. I'd forgotten how tiny a tea glass can look in a man's hand. I walked on. Here and there I recognized a house, a fragment of wall full of holes, the barber's shop, the square with the acacias, the cracked concrete pipes for the well that was never dug.

The road forked, and I bore left onto the Street of the Three Widows. I didn't recognize anything here any more. The road was freshly tarred, but the tar had split in the heat and its black wounds bulged open. My parents' house had vanished. Three cars were parked on the empty plot, which was littered with stones. The back of the parking lot was marked by a low, half-derelict wall. I couldn't tell if it was our garden wall or the remains of the bedroom. I sat down on one of the sections. The sun was high; everything was drenched in its blinding white light. I couldn't remember what I'd intended to do. I think I had wanted to scatter my parents' ashes over the grass in their garden. I'd thought someone was sure to be living in the house, so I would have to be quick, a swift movement of my hand in the wind. But there was no wind, no garden and no house. There was just a parking lot and the heat.

Hard to say how long I sat there. Eventually I got up, took the two little pouches from the pocket of my shirt and scattered the ashes on the stony surface. They left no trace, seeming simply to dissolve into the hot ground. I believe I wept, but I'm not sure. Later, a man appeared. He nodded at me, got into one of the cars and drove off. I stood and listened to the sound of the engine until it faded away. My forehead was burning, and there was a rushing in my ears. I longed for shade and quiet. I think I longed for home.

Back on the plane, I saw the desert far below, and later the sea, a vast glittering streaked with furrows. We were flying into the evening, and although the engines were roaring I could feel the silence and peace that surrounded us. I leaned back my head and closed my eyes. I thought of the day to come. The cool morning air. The scent of fruit in the darkness of the shop and the rattle of the shutters. I would order pointed peppers and yellow plums. I would unroll my father's old rug and clean off the dirt that had fallen from the turnip sacks I shook out so often on account of the damp and the mould.

When you stood in the fire, and the hot ash was searing your skin, did you see God, Father Hoberg?

Herm Leydicke

Can you hear me? Do you hear?

You were fifteen when my time came. How old are you now? Time doesn't exist here. But let's assume you still have a good long while to go. I have to assume this, because otherwise none of what I have to say to you would make any sense. You see, there are a few things I'd like to get off my chest. I wish I'd said them to you when I was still alive. I wish someone had said them to me. Perhaps there were things I would have done differently. Though probably not.

I wasn't a clever man. That's no secret. Your mother knew it. I knew it, too. I've seen some things, but that doesn't count for much. No amount of experience will help you if you don't have the wit to think things through and draw useful conclusions. Or if you no longer have the strength to haul your backside out of the armchair. Very few old people are wise; the majority are just old. And I was definitely part of the majority.

If I'd understood (I don't mean *known*, but really *understood*) that everything passes so quickly, there are things I would have spared myself. But now my time's up, so I like to think I might at least be able to spare you some of them. You didn't have the best start in life, and I'm probably not entirely blameless in that. But you can't change the past. And you're alive, at least. That's more than anyone can ask for. I see I'm starting to blather on. So I'm just going to tell you a few things. What you do with them is up to you.

1. Don't bother trying to find the right woman. She doesn't exist. As soon as you think you've found the right woman, she'll turn out to be wrong. You can try to find enough that's right about the wrong woman for it still to be fun. But that's all.

2. There probably isn't a God.

3. If, though, for some reason God does actually exist (although there's really very little to support this conclusion), then maybe there's also a possibility of finding the right woman.

4. The right woman is a woman with guts. She's the one whose feet you hear crunching the gravel before she's even turned the corner. One who can take an apple and coax a pigeon down from the gutter. She's a woman in a yellow skirt who has her wits about her, a laugh that's

much too loud, red fingernails, but unpainted toes. She carries a knife in her handbag, a salt shaker and a tiny collapsible bronze ashtray; she needs the ashtray, because she's a woman who smokes filterless cigarettes. She's a woman of principle, which she sets aside if need be. One who pounds the steering wheel with her fist until the varnish splinters off her fingernails. A woman who doesn't tell you; one who isn't ashamed. Who cries at the cinema, but never, never, never watches her figure. Who likes unpeeled potatoes and secretly believes in the Mother of God; one who looks after your affairs and is even happier looking after her own. The right woman is one who knows what love is, and who, if she finds one day that she's forgotten, makes it short and sweet.

5. These are just ideas. Forget it.

6. Forget what they tell you about drinking, too, by the way. It can be nice. It can take you out of yourself. And it can calm you down when you need it. Alcohol isn't a devil. The devil is the fat fly that buzzes around your room on a summer night and won't let you sleep. Alcohol is just a chemical compound; besides, it's not impossible that you're able to control it. But if you find yourself sitting at the bar and the panelling comes alive and there are little creatures darting about under the bar stools, order another. It won't make any difference.

7. Is the house still standing? You should paint it. When I last painted it, you weren't even two years old. It was summer, and hot, and I burned my bum easing backwards over the roof. You were in the garden, and I could see you picking the heads off the rosebush one by one. I wonder why you were down there on your own, on that hot day that smelled of wood paint and grass. Anyway: if you don't want the house to rot, you should paint it. But remember to sand the wood first. You need eighty-grit sandpaper. At least. After that, primer. Linseed oil is very good, too. Then start. Two or three coats of paint. And don't let anyone persuade you to use a roller. Brushes are better.

8. Go down to the cellar. In the corner is the locker with the garden tools. Push it aside and lift up the granite slab underneath. There's a metal box in the hole. Everything you find in it belongs to you. Including the photos.

9. There may be a war. There's always a war somewhere, so why not here? There's always some lunatic somewhere sitting at a button and fiddling with it. And it always takes a while for people to realize that he's crazy. And I don't mean crazy like Father Hoberg or Richard Regnier, who sometimes used to sit on the grass after work talking to the birds. I mean real madness. Madness that wears a tie and polished shoes. That nods at the bathroom mirror in the evening and can't stop laughing because it knows

it's won again, it can't lose, because it has nothing to lose. It's a madness whose fingers are short and thin, too small to hurt another man but just big enough to press a button. Perhaps someone will recognize this madness, but by then it will be too late. So there may be a war. Now listen. No matter what they whisper to or yell at you, what they tempt or threaten you with: it's not your war. You didn't come into this world to end up lying in the mud somewhere with your belly split open. *It's not your war.*

10. When you sit at the window in the morning and see the cars driving down the approach road outside, think about how lucky you are. You've got through the night, and you know more or less what to expect from the day. It's not much, and that's what's good about it. You put your bare feet on the window ledge and feel the draught on your toes. A piece of plastic film hangs from the window frame and moves as though it were alive. You see your toes curling and stretching, and winter is still a long way off.

11. Trust no doctors.

12. Think of the dead and forgive them.

13. Look for friends. You can find them anywhere. On the street. On the next corner. At the petrol station, while

you're trying to unscrew the valve on your tyre. Any-where. I think the secret is: you've got to be *interested*. The best friend I ever had in my life was my father. How is that possible? He was thirty-one years older than me.

14. Go to your mother and put your hand on her cheek. Stay like that for a moment. I never did, and that was a mistake.

15. Say: I love you! I know that to your ears it sounds idiotic and wrong. But not to theirs. I never said it. No idea why. I couldn't. They asked me to. They expected it. They demanded it, again and again, but I couldn't. They often said it. I love you! And then they wanted to hear it from me. I took the view that love wasn't something you bar-tered, and I never said it. Not once. And that was almost certainly the biggest mistake of all.

Lennie Martin

It's not as if I was stupid and couldn't learn. I just didn't want to. 'Lennie Martin, you have no willpower. You have no drive. You're lazier than the laziest couch potato rotting in the dampest cellar in town,' said my teacher. I never set much store by her opinion, but she was right about this. I dropped out of school and gave work a go. I scrubbed the concrete forecourt of Kobielski's car showroom and dragged myself across fields yanking potatoes out of the earth. Sometimes I helped the Arab with his vegetables. We piled up crates and cleaned apples and melons with a soft cloth until they shone like the ones on the pub fruit machine. I never stuck at anything for more than a few weeks. Back then, I was convinced I had no staying power. Actually, staying power was pretty much the only thing I did have in life.

I was living in a basement at the time, right behind the church. I didn't plan on staying there long, and I kept my things in a wooden crate so that when I got the chance I could carry them to a better apartment with minimal effort. The room was tiny and damp. The damp crept into my bones, and sometimes in the morning I was so stiff I could hardly get out of bed. Often I would lie under the blanket for hours with my knees pulled up to my chest, waiting, I don't know what for.

As soon as I had any money I would spend every evening in the Golden Moon, sitting at that counter pockmarked with cigarette burns. When you glanced in the mirror behind the bar, a row of gloomy faces stared back at you. There were always three or four men sitting there, playing cards or listening to records on the jukebox. We didn't talk much, and I think that was how we all liked it.

I remember one evening in winter. I'd spent the whole day hacking ice a centimetre thick off Kobielski's forecourt, and I was sitting at the bar, dog-tired. Beside me sat a man I only knew by sight. We were staring out of the window at the street, where snow was whirling in the light from the streetlamp, and all of a sudden he started telling me about his life. He said he had certainly had his chances, but he had just lacked courage. 'You take your eye off the ball just once, and before you know it it's all over,' he kept saying. He said it without bitterness, without any discernible expression on his face or in his voice. And perhaps this was what bothered me. Suddenly I no longer had any idea why I was sitting there or what I even wanted from life. I was filled with anger of a kind I'd never felt before. At this man, at myself, at life in general. Perhaps I'd just had too much to drink. In any case, I interrupted him and said, 'I'm going to smash my head in.'

'What?' he said.

'I'm just going to.'

'Leave it,' he said, but it was too late. I slammed my forehead down on the damp wooden counter. I felt no pain, but when I looked up again I saw the blood on my face in the mirror.

'It's fine,' I said.

The following year, things changed. It was a scorching hot summer. It was only when the sun went down that you could breathe and people would venture out into the open again. There was an event on the outskirts of town. The car show-room was celebrating its fifteenth anniversary, and Kobielski had invited a few customers to a party, along with current and former employees. Everyone was standing under the canopy roof of the brightly lit sales hall, holding paper cups and plates. It was a Friday; most of them had just been paid, and their faces shone with eager anticipation of the evening.

I was standing with my back to the shop window, leaning against it and looking out at the forecourt, where the chains of coloured light bulbs strung from the roof to the main entrance were reflected in puddles of oil, when suddenly she was standing there beside me. 'Good evening,' she said. 'I'm Louise.'

I thought that name was far too posh for a small-town girl, and said so. She laughed and asked what was so interesting out on the forecourt. Nothing, I said, just light bulbs. Still, she said, light bulbs were better than nothing. True, I said, and they're nice and colourful. We laughed, had a few glasses of wine, and it all felt good, as if it had never been any other way. At one point she raised her hand and pushed a lock of hair behind my ear. She only did it in passing, but when I felt her fingers on my temple I jumped, and I realized how long it had been since anyone had touched me.

Around midnight, Kobielski climbed onto the load bed of a 504 pickup and made a speech. He'd had a few too many, and very little of what he said made sense, but he was so moved by his own words that they brought tears to his eyes. After that he let off a few fireworks, and as the rockets soared into the sky, Louise and I put our arms around each other, and it was as if the puddles of oil were exploding. As if the forecourt and everything around it were bursting into colourful flames.

Later, alone in my basement, I could still feel her fingers on my temple. I thought of her, and it was so lovely, and at the same time I could have smashed in the walls around me for sheer loneliness.

We saw each other again. We walked through the streets,

sat in Lehmkuhl's café or kissed under the chestnuts in the park, and after a few weeks she took me back to the little apartment where she lived with her grandmother. I think I went around with a grin on my face all day. I was spending time with a girl I might never be without again, and it felt good.

Three months after the evening at Kobielski's, I packed up the crate with my things and moved in with Louise. Her grandmother, a silent old woman who sat on the window seat all day, couldn't stand me. She had a gift for looking straight at me and ignoring me at the same time. But I didn't care. I was with her granddaughter; I had nothing to do with her.

Louise wasn't exactly what you'd call a beauty. She was quite thin, with black hair and huge eyes that bulged in their sockets. But her forehead was high and smooth, and occasionally something seemed to pass over it like a shadow. I always liked to look at her. Her face. Her hands. The way she moved. Once, when we were lying in bed, I said to her, 'Would you walk up and down for me?'

'What do you mean?' she asked.

'Just a few steps across the room?'

She got up and walked up and down in front of me. I watched her for a while, then we both burst out laughing and she threw herself on top of me and I buried my face in her body and inhaled her scent.

I liked her voice, too. It had a very special timbre, and

there was something rough and raw about it when she was preoccupied. Louise often talked about her work at the Black Buck. She cleaned the rooms there, made coffee and ironed the little crocheted doilies yellowed by cigarette smoke. She picked up quite a bit about the guests, and had some very odd experiences, but really I just wanted to listen to her voice and watch her lips move as she talked.

Once in a while we'd sit on the sofa and watch a film on TV, but she would fall asleep every time. Her head would drop onto my shoulder, and I could gaze at her face as long as I liked.

I would have been happy for things to carry on like this for ever. But then her grandmother died. We found her one morning on the floor in front of the window seat. Her arm was twisted oddly underneath her torso, and her head was propped against the chair leg, her eyes open. When we walked into the room it looked as if she was staring at us.

I didn't know how to deal with Louise's grief. I felt useless around her. I wanted to do something for her, but a few days later, when I started tidying up, she planted herself in my way.

'What are you doing?' she asked.

'I'm taking this stuff out.'

'Leave those things where they are!'

She stood in front of me, hands on hips, looking me dead in the eye. I'd never seen her like this. For the first time since we'd met, she seemed like a stranger.

'OK,' I said. 'Don't get in a state.'

'I'm not getting in a state. And I want you to start looking for work. Gran's pension's gone now. The money from the Black Buck won't be enough.'

'OK.'

'Promise me.'

I got a job at the town hall, or rather in the parks and gardens department, where I worked with Richard Regnier. We drove all around town in a clapped-out van, pruning trees, clearing weeds from flowerbeds or pulling them out of the gaps between paving stones. I didn't know Regnier well; we'd crossed paths here and there, and I'd seen him a couple of times in the Golden Moon. I remember him setting aside his rake in the town park one day, pulling down his trousers and squatting under a golden willow. 'Out of the earth, the man,' he said, giving me a serious look. 'Out of the man, the earth.' I think he was a bit mad.

To begin with it was hard. My whole body ached. The pain started in my back; it radiated out over my hips, down to my knees, and up over my shoulders and arms, right to the tips of my fingers. There were open blisters on my hands, and the dirt seemed to eat its way into every pore. It grew easier with time; I got used to the hard labour, and there were even days in spring and late summer when I liked it.

One evening, Regnier insisted on inviting me for a beer.

I hadn't been to the Moon for ages, and when we walked in, in our filthy overalls, I was curious to see whether the same men were still sitting there, or whether some of them, at least, had put it behind them. They were all still there; that is, they looked like the same men, sitting in their seats and staring into their glasses.

But something was different. It was the light. The whole room was lit up. It moved, pulsed, darted across a hunched back, a soot-blackened forehead, trembled red and green and yellow in a half-empty beer glass. The light was coming from a slot machine that stood in the corner between the bar and the wall. It was as tall as a man and about a metre wide, and the front was studded with little flickering, blinking lights. I didn't know it back then, but it was just an old-fashioned Lucky Deal, one of the first models, a screen, no handle, four rows and a rainbow sun in the middle.

We sat at the counter and ordered beers. We were tired and didn't have much to say to each other. The colours from the little lights twinkled in my beer. The dots and blobs spun and danced in the glass like a shoal of tiny colourful fish.

I walked over to the corner. The Lucky Deal chuckled. I put my hand on its side. The wood was warm; it vibrated beneath my fingers. For a moment I saw my face reflected in the screen, pale and shadowy, as if underwater. I put a couple of coins in the slot and pressed the button. Instantly the reels were set in motion; the symbols raced off. Then, one after another, with a soft sound, they stopped: the melon, the seven, the bell, the coin.

I pressed the button again. And again, and again. I fetched a bar stool and some more coins. The light, the sounds, the flickering screen all made me nervous. I jiggled my legs and chinked the coins in my pocket. 'Come on,' I said to the reels in front of me. 'Get on with it!' Then I won nine times the amount I'd put in. The machine went crazy, everything blinked and flashed and it played a shrill fanfare. I burst out laughing. My heart was racing; it felt as if the wooden floor was swaying under the stool, and my hand shook as I pressed the button for another go.

Later, Regnier appeared at my side. 'It's time,' he said.

'I'm staying,' I said.

Regnier sighed. 'Listen,' he said, with an effort, as if chewing on a tough lump of food. 'Listen.' But he didn't say anything else, and when I didn't say anything either, and pressed the button, which felt warm and familiar now, he turned and left.

My winning streak came right at the start, and it was fantastic. As soon as I finished work I would head for the Moon, and I'd take home winnings almost every night. I couldn't believe it: for the first time in my life I felt that I'd found something. It may sound strange, but the moment I stood in front of the Lucky Deal I felt *right*.

I think it felt like love.

They weren't huge sums of money, but I won so often that one day I bought Louise a necklace of polished red stones. I don't know what kind of stones they were, but they looked as if they were glowing from the inside out. I put the necklace around her neck, and she looked at me with a gaze that pierced my heart. That evening, I was convinced that nothing else could hurt us.

But the Lucky Deal soon began to bore me. I fancied something new, and I wasn't winning as much, either. I'd heard there was an amusement arcade in the leisure centre they'd built on that field on the outskirts of town. I took the bus and went there.

The centre was a massively oversized glass and concrete box, and I didn't mean to stay long. But when I found the casino in the arcade in the basement and stepped through its doors, I got a shock. Everything in there was excessive: the flashing, blinking, shining, humming, beeping, yowling and screeching, an inconceivable chaos of lights, sounds, voices and music. I stood on a carpet peppered with cigarette burns, feeling like the Rocket Man in a film I'd seen with Louise: lost and secure at the same time in the infinite loneliness of the universe.

I went almost every night. Sometimes I borrowed the van and drove out there still in my work clothes. I'd been bitten by the bug. During the day, standing in the greenery somewhere, I was already thinking about the slot machines:

the Six Bomb, the Cash Crazy or the Diamond Seven. I'd be hoeing the weeds and the corn poppy would start blinking in front of my eyes like the lights on the big Lucky Chambers.

Then I began to lose. It was hardly worth mentioning at first, but it soon mounted up. I should have known what to do. But I took it personally: I saw the losses as defeats, and I started talking to the machines. I spoke to them, beseeched them, begged and pleaded with them, yelled and screamed at them. I upped my stake and lost. I used a system and lost. I took risks and lost. I kept count as the odds went into reverse, slowly at first, then faster and faster. There were still good days, but they just made it worse, because they restored my faith. I kept playing and lost. I lost more than I would ever have thought possible.

Things would look up again. I knew I would win. I'd lost my way; I just needed to be a bit patient and I'd find it again. I started running up debts. I borrowed money from everyone I met. You'll get it back, I told people. Just give me a little time and you'll get it all back!

When they stopped believing me, I started stealing. Whenever an opportunity presented itself, I would slip a few coins or notes into my pocket, and one night I climbed into the town hall through a basement window and used my brush hook to break open the municipal coffers.

They didn't catch me until I tried to sell the van. I'd registered it as stolen and hidden it under a tarpaulin at the back of the old greenhouse by the approach road. I wanted to offload it through a contact from the amusement arcade. The contact had a big mouth, the tarpaulin was carried away by the wind, and the story got out.

The town hall didn't press charges; I think Regnier put in a word for me. But they threw me out. After I'd hung up my overalls in the locker, we shook hands. 'All the best. I think it's going to rain tomorrow,' he said, scratching his head.

News got around. Kobielski wouldn't even let me scrub the pavement any more. So I went back to slaving in the fields and stacking vegetable crates. And I went to the Golden Moon, like in the old days. The Lucky Deal stood in the corner. I thought it looked shabby, all scratched and worn. But it was ringing, beeping and flashing, and it was as if an old friend was there waiting for me.

I don't know when exactly I lost Louise. I think our time was already up when I still thought things could carry on for ever as they were. But perhaps I didn't even think that. In the morning I would often pretend to be asleep. I couldn't wait for her to go out of the house and leave me in peace. Later, in front of the machine, I would hardly think of her. There were moments when her face seemed to appear on the screen, and I knew then that I still loved her. But as soon as the reels started spinning, it was gone.

By the time I got home she'd usually gone to bed, and I was glad. Sometimes, though, she would still be sitting on the sofa, watching the late-night film. I would sit beside her, put my arm around her and think: please don't say anything! Please don't say anything now, let's just sit here and watch the rest of this film, please!

And every time she would start. I was wrong if I thought she was the kind of woman who meddled in other people's affairs. 'Don't think I want to tell you what to do,' she said. 'I don't want to change you. I'd just like to understand you. If I'm living with you, I'd like at least to have some idea of who you are and what the hell is going on in your head!'

She could really fly into a rage at moments like these. She would pace up and down, talking loudly, wave her arms around, abruptly change direction, stop, stare me in the face, then pace about some more. By the light of the television it looked as if she was doing a crazy dance.

One evening, a little after Christmas, I was later than usual. It was cold; out on the street a biting wind was blowing away the light, dry snow of the past few days. I'd had a small win, and was looking forward to getting home; oddly enough, I was hoping Louise would still be awake and that things might resolve themselves tonight. I walked through the snow, heard the coins jingling in my trouser pocket, and imagined how it would be to stroke the back of her neck.

She was sitting on the sofa. The TV was off, and I could see that she'd been crying.

'I'd like you to stop,' she said.

'Stop what?'

'Take off your coat.'

'What am I supposed to stop?' I asked again. I stood there, in the middle of the room, and felt as if my shoes were nailed to the floor. My hands were cold and heavy. The coat dripped and dripped.

She said, 'I want you to decide. Either you stop, or you leave.'

I laughed out loud. It was an angry laugh, abrupt and quiet. I felt betrayed. Suddenly I felt heat behind my eyes, and my shoulders tensed.

'Don't do it,' she said quietly. She stared at her hands in her lap and shook her head slowly. The clock ticked on the wall above the spot where her grandmother had always sat.

'Louise,' I said.

She raised her head and looked at me. 'Leave,' she said. 'Please, just leave now.'

I couldn't speak. But what could I have said? At first I thought perhaps we could get through it somehow; then I realized it was too late. I loved her, but she made me choose. And that was ridiculous, because there was no choice.

As I closed the door behind me, I heard her in there, sobbing. It was like the wail of an animal, a noise like nothing I'd ever heard before.

*

And that's it. About three years later I got a letter. A card in an envelope, in fact, closely covered with her neat handwriting. She wrote that she had left town and was now living with a man called Stephen. I should come and visit them sometime. Stephen would fire up the grill, we'd eat sausages and potatoes and talk, or just sit there and enjoy the garden. Enjoy the garden? I imagined how they lived, in a little house with a gravel drive, a pear tree and a juniper hedge. It was a strange thought. She didn't know the first thing about plants and found the little creatures under the leaves disgusting. Stephen would have to deal with the greenery by himself.

The day Louise's card arrived, I went to the Golden Moon. I still had a few coins. I sat down at the Lucky Deal and began to play. And that's the thing: the reels keep spinning as long as you just keep pressing the button. You play. You up the stake. You win a few times. Then you lose. But you keep going. You always keep on going.

Louise Trattner

It smells of men. Of their breath, their saliva, their sweat, of all that they've shed in the night. The beds are still warm, the covers rumpled. There are damp patches on the sheets. Some look like islands, others like heads. I picture them lying there. Their sweaty bodies trying to curl up in this nest after a day of defeats. They've travelled across the country in their patent-leather shoes with their suitcases on wheels, they've sat in corridors and rooms and cheap pub restaurants, stood at bus stops and in doorways, they've rushed and run, talked and talked, hunched and smiling and furtive, always ready for whatever might happen, only to crawl at last into a cold, unfamiliar bed. But now the dreams come. They're dreams of power and ruin, conquest and disintegration, train stations and refreshment kiosks, endless rows of empty wooden benches, and a woman's white arm dangling from a train window like a scrap of cloth.

Do you know why I'm so familiar with these men's dreams, Lennie? They told them to me.

Do you remember Kobielski's? You were leaning against the window, the showroom full of expensive cars all lit up behind you. You looked good. Your whole stance expressed a kind of nonchalance, a casual indifference to the world. You'd lowered your head; your face was in shadow. That made you seem mysterious, but at the same time I felt I recognized you. Because the truth is: it was a mistake. I thought you were someone else, that's why I spoke to you. Maybe I should have cleared that up right away, but you were funny and I was lonely. Or maybe I just thought you were funny *because* I was lonely. Whatever – it makes no difference. Later, when Kobielski let off his fireworks, we'd already been leaning against the window for a while, shoulder to shoulder, staring out into the exploding night.

They warned me about you. All the women I knew, and most of the men. My grandmother said, be careful, that man is bad for you. I said, don't worry, I'm a grown-up. No one's ever grown-up enough for love, she said. I said, Gran, you're old. You had your experiences, but your experiences aren't mine, do you understand? She just looked at me with her old, grey eyes.

So you got it wrong when you thought it was *you* I meant that evening. You often got it wrong.

How many times did you think I'd fallen asleep on the

sofa with my head on your shoulder? I never slept, not once. I just closed my eyes. I knew you would look at my face. I could feel your gaze, and I knew you wouldn't dare move until I opened my eyes again. It was my way of holding on to you, at least until the film was over.

Because that's also the truth: I wanted you. You can't explain these things. It's as if you jump into a river even though you know it flows into an abyss. Only suicides and lovers know what that's like. I wanted you, and I got you. I jumped. And it was nice to drift along with you for a while.

I never told you, but I saw you, once. Only one time. I'd had enough of waiting for you and I went out in the middle of the night. The town was in darkness. The only light on the street came from the window of the Golden Moon. I saw you standing in front of that machine. Your fingers calmly, rhythmically pressing coins into the slot. Your foot, beating time on the floorboards. And I saw your face, with the reflections of the little lights skimming across it. I wanted to go to you, but I couldn't move; I stayed outside on the street. What was so disconcerting was that you looked happy. You still looked as good as you did that night at Kobielski's, yet you were more of a stranger to me than ever before. You were a good-looking, happy stranger. I watched you for half an hour or more, and then I went home.

I don't know what it was that made me carry on. Or rather, I do know: it was the fear of being alone. And my own stubbornness. I became stupidly determined to show everyone. I wanted to prove to them that they'd been wrong, that their experiences had nothing to do with mine, and not every blasted river has to end in a blasted abyss.

Do you remember the necklace with the red stones that you laid out for me on the bed? When I opened my eyes, I thought for a moment that there was blood on the pillow. You put the necklace around my neck. They were glass stones. Cool, smooth, cheap glass. I didn't say anything. I didn't say anything, either, when one day the necklace was gone. Or when my grandmother's silver ring suddenly couldn't be found. Not a word when coins and notes went missing from my bag. Did you ever actually wonder where I got hold of so much money? Why it was sometimes loose in my handbag? How much do you think a chambermaid earns in a cheap hotel like the Black Buck? Not enough, Lennie.

But I was determined. And there were the men in the tangled beds, with their tangled dreams. I can't remember a single one of the many words they whispered in my ear, not a single name, and even the memory of their faces faded before I left the room. Only the smell remained.

Then again, it could have been worse. I forgave you your lies. The stealing. And did you really think I didn't know that your job wasn't all about clipping rosebuds? Could you seriously have thought that, in all those years, I never once saw you rinsing out waste bins or scratching dried dogshit off the pavement?

I've forgiven you, Lennie. But I couldn't forgive myself. I'm not talking about the lost time. You can't lose time. I lost my dignity. Or rather: I gave it away. I discarded my dignity like an old coat.

The night you left there was a film on TV. It was about a pilot who falls in love with a dark-eyed smuggler in Puerto Rico and gets into trouble on her account. The pilot couldn't sleep because of the heat, and kept stroking his thumb across his moustache. I don't remember anything else. I cried all through the film. I sobbed and screamed into the cushions. I was furious. I couldn't understand what had happened. I thought of my grandmother and all the others. I hated the lot of them, and I hated myself. But most of all I hated you, Lennie.

Eventually the fit passed. The film had finished and I could hear the news from underneath my blanket; it seemed to be coming from a long way off. Something inside me had broken, or snapped, and I knew that I would never have to see you in the Golden Moon again, with that bright happiness in your face.

Stephen was a good man. He'd decided that I was the one, and I was tired and wanted someone I could lean on. His salary was enough for both of us, and I was able to give up the Black Buck. I wanted to take care of the garden. The plants all died, one after another, and I said to Stephen, it's probably because of the soil or the rain or the dirty air or something. He said, you're probably right, and we concreted over two-thirds of the lawn. At least the pear tree bloomed. Its blossom was delicate and white, and in spring, when we opened the windows, the house filled with its scent.

I bet you think I'm still alive. You never did have much imagination. Perhaps you think that right at this moment I'm standing beside your grave with big fat tears in my eyes or something. Wrong again.

Do you remember the card I sent you? I wrote it one evening in April. It was pelting down outside. I sat at the kitchen table, wrote the card, and felt better and freer than I had in ages. When I'd finished I got up and went over to the window. The pear tree was rustling in the rain. The next morning I felt too weak to get up, and barely a month later I was dead. Something had been eating me up inside for a long time. Stephen stayed with me till the end. He sat beside my bed, and I saw his face get paler by the day, until finally you couldn't distinguish it in the chalk-white brightness of the room. I have hardly any recollection of those days and nights. One of my last memories was of your hands, Lennie. Your fingers smelled of earth.

Gerda Baehr

I lie here and think of you. Or perhaps I'm just dreaming of you; it makes no difference. I know that today is Sunday, because there's a lot of activity up above. Before, on Sundays, we would sometimes stay in bed; we would make love and then just lie quietly. Long before that, I wouldn't have thought it was possible to have so much fun with a fat man. We didn't spend all day in bed, of course. No one does that. But outdoors was nice as well. A Sunday without you was incomplete. Making love with you, then lying beside you, in bed, in the grass, in the snow. That was everything.

K. P. Lindow

A little boy is sitting in front of his radio in the garden. He hears a song and starts to cry. He whimpers and sobs. Not because the song is so sad. He whimpers and sobs because it will soon be over.

It's summer. Wasps are coming into the house. They've hatched too early, and dozens of them buzz about the room, above the table, at the window, before dying. My mother sweeps them into her little dustpan; my father climbs onto the garage roof to look for the nest. He wants to smoke it out. I liked the wasps. I wasn't afraid that one of them might sting. I was afraid of other things. To me, the wasps were innocent. They were angels, now small and curled and dead and trickling into my mother's dustpan.

Collected: stones, little lumps of sulphur, milk teeth, snail shells, bits of dirt, pictures of nude women, dead people's names, rubber bands (all colours except red), corkscrews, beer mats, stamps, spectacle lenses, swearwords, revenge fantasies.

Revenge fantasies: discover my parents' secrets and circulate them by way of anonymous letters. Stretch a thin wire across Marktstrasse to decapitate my maths teacher as he cycles past. Blow up various buildings. Win her back, only to leave her again. Self-immolation on the town hall square. Gouge out Father's eyes. Hack Mother to pieces. Renounce revenge, thereby shaming the enemy with goodness and generosity and leaving him in a swamp of his own villainy.

My hands, small, soft, pink balls, strike the carpet. Then the building blocks. The fire station. All of it must be destroyed. All of it must dissolve in my hot, wet, bubbling anger. My hands do what I want. They strike the grown-ups' words dead before they can reach my ears. They are my friends, the only ones I have.

The same hands (are they really the same?), seventy years on. I stare at them, the blotches, the wrinkles, the hairs, the scars. What happened? They lie on a yellow plastic tablecloth, fingers intertwined like gnarled roots. Praying came to them after all, with age. Or rather, pleading. Please give me. Please let me. Please grant me. Please. Please!

Gradually, imperceptibly, the longing for first times transforms into hoping for last ones.

All those plastic tablecloths. In the attic. In the garden. In school. In the back room. In the common room. In the guest house. At the neighbours'. At the police station. At the fire station. At everyone else's house. In the hospital. In the quiet room. In the basement.

Spring festival. The Chinese lanterns sway in the wind, and three fights break out before it even gets dark. Everything's the same as always, then suddenly completely different. A yellow skirt. A laugh. A pebble in a shoe. Falling in love is inflammation. More courage is needed to take her hand than, later, to undress in front of her. But at least there's no need for much conversation just yet.

Let's leave the window open tonight. – The cats will watch us. – Fine by me: come here! I love her. I love her stomach. Her behind. Her face. Her voice. I love everything she says and does. We vanquished Death that night. And the cats had fun.

Then it was over. Yet nothing happened. There wasn't even another man. She just left. There were reasons that she stacked up in front of me like bricks. I heard them and forgot them again. She packed her things and moved in with her mother. Later, she left town. We hugged each other good-bye, and she said: I'll call you.

Another collection: moments with her. Yellow summer days. The wet hamster on the mat. The feet in the shoebox. Three deodorants for the price of one. Smothered laughter. The business with the blackbird. The black smoke above the poplars. Us under the tree. On the sofa. On the kitchen table. In the grass. In the field. In bed.

Our table is now my table again.

There were others afterwards, of course. It was never the same, but who wants that, anyway? And later on I had a cat. He was old, his fur was dull and mangy, his tail had several kinks in it and one of his back legs protruded stiffly from the hip like a stick. His right eye was cloudy and moved only slowly. Perhaps it was blind. But his teeth were yellow and healthy and he could still run like a youngster, despite his damaged leg. We liked each other right from the start. He came up to me and slunk around my trouser legs. He was in bad condition, skinny and weak, and it took a while to feed him up. What didn't go away was his stench. There was nothing to be done about it. He stank like a dustbin. I got used to it, though, in time. It was only after he died that I noticed the scent of springtime and the smell of my own body again.

The Field

I think I talked to that cat more than I did to most people.

The blue-black night sky. Drunks beneath the window, bellowing and roaring after their friends or after their own yearnings. Then silence again. A shadow across the roof. Apparently there are bats in the town hall again, the first in decades. The phone rings. It stops again. Your stomach grumbles. There's half a bread roll on the table. But the table is far away. Everything is far away. Only the bat is sitting on your forehead. It sits there and looks at you and covers your face with its wings.

It's a strange business, letting go. A tooth falls out of my mouth as I'm washing. It never hurt, or even wobbled. Now it's lying in the washbasin, ground down and yellow, stained with brown. It's a traitor. At least I still have seven. I'm going to give them names.

Father's steps in the hall. The smell of Mother's fur hat. The doctor. The night nurses' voices. The railway. Our fingers in the disgusting velvety gap between the cushions of the cinema seats. Bus journeys. Dark winter evenings. Spilled milk on the kitchen floor. Falls. Wounds. Scars. Her arms. Her feet. Her forehead. The box of building blocks in the dustbin. Biscuits. Apples. Bread and butter. Thirteen glasses still aren't enough. Dead birds outside the front door. A dying wasp like a droning top on the window ledge. Distant music. Death comes like a wind. It picks you up. It carries you away.

How do I know this? I don't know.

Stephanie Stanek

I saw the church burn. It was a warm autumn morning. I was already old by then, and restlessness drove me outdoors very early. I walked through the streets and soon heard the crackling of the flames. The church was burning bright, and the priest's shadowy form could be seen through the open door, standing amid the billowing smoke with outstretched arms as the sparks rained down. People came running. They screamed. Then the fire brigade arrived. The priest's back was blackened when they carried him out and laid him on a stretcher. The church burned to the ground. Sparks hung in the twigs of the chestnut tree like little electric lights. They looked pretty. My heart hurt, because of the memories. Later, the church was rebuilt, but I didn't live to see the topping-out ceremony.

The night I died the sky clouded over, and not long afterwards it began to snow. It was cold. At the funeral, one of the gravediggers slipped and nearly fell into the open grave. Not many people came. Lotte. My granddaughter Louise. Three women. A priest I didn't know. He said, 'Lie down and rest, for you were tired,' and it snowed and snowed.

I've seen a lot of clergymen, but I didn't like any of them. I mistrusted them. I liked going to church, but never to confession. I knew that even if God forgave me, I couldn't forgive myself.

But the priest was right: I was tired. My journey had been a long one. I remember how it began. The village, the name of which I do not like to say aloud. The animals. The smell of burnt straw, horse dung and spring sunshine. The skeletal winter trees. A hare without eyes, frozen stiff in the bushes. Meat at Christmas. My parents. Papa's boots. The forest. The snow. So much snow.

The front was already within earshot, and the forest on the horizon seemed to be glowing. When they came and broke down the door, I was crouching in the damp straw beside the cow with my little Lotte. They took away my parents and all that we had. Our house disappeared in the last of the fires.

For a while we were able to hide at our neighbour's. There were floorboards in her larder that we could take up and crawl underneath. They came every day, looking for meat, clothes and women. We lay there silently as they crashed about the house above us in their winter boots. I held Lotte inside my coat and felt her warm breath on my belly.

I don't understand why they took our neighbour. She was just an old woman. Perhaps she did something stupid; perhaps they came in the dark and somebody made a mistake. Anyway, one day she was gone and they found us. But we were lucky. We were put in a group of women, children and old men. Everyone was given armbands, and we all walked to the train station together. My little girl waved when the train pulled in. I could see through a hatch as we set off. The platform was bathed in sunlight. A few men laughed and shouted something at me as the train began to move. A woman's brown shoe lay on the platform edge.

We spent the first part of the journey in the goods wagon. It was so cramped that we had to take turns sitting down, but somehow we managed. Shortly before the border the train stopped and we continued on foot. When we had crossed the border, we tore off the armbands and set light to them. Many people were laughing as if they'd gone mad. One woman threw her armband on the ground and jumped and danced on it. I sat down on a rock and exhaled. My life after that, my whole life after that brief moment on the rock at the border, was one long exhalation.

We joined the trek. We slept under carts, in barns, in open fields. The nights were cold and we often went hungry. When we got the chance, we took onions and potatoes from the fields. We knew we were thieves, but we felt no remorse.

There were camphor injections against typhus, but

camphor makes people mad; I knew that, and stopped. In a delirious fever, I saw a horse. It was standing calmly on the horizon, carrying the red sun on its back. Black angels sat in the trees by the roadside.

I'd always known how strong Lotte was. She was only six, but she could walk like a big girl. Her legs were brown and smooth under the dust from the road. We walked side by side, holding hands. One day we'll get there. That's what I told her. We'll arrive and then we'll rest. Right now, we have to keep walking. On and on, towards the west, one step at a time, between the hordes of others in front of us and behind, their numbers dwindling every day. One day we'll get there and we'll rest.

It took longer than we were told. It seemed there wasn't much room in the country, and we were sent here, there and everywhere. Eventually we arrived in Paulstadt. Supposedly we had a relative here, but I never found him. Perhaps I'd just imagined it.

In the early days we lived in the coal cellar under Buxter's butcher's shop. The cellar was dark and cold, but the coal drew the dampness out of the air, and sometimes the butcher gave us a few bones or an offcut for our soup.

Lotte never met her father. I heard later that by the time his letters reached us he was long since dead. She never met him, so she didn't miss him, either, which was lucky for her. We stayed in Paulstadt. There was no way back.

There was work, first in the fields, later in Frau Klausner's sweet and chocolate shop, where I served the customers. I liked the work, and Lotte grew up nicely. She got a bit fat on all the broken chocolate. But she found a husband, and brought Louise into the world. Later, she left town for a job elsewhere. Louise had a mind of her own and stayed with me; and I watched her become a woman, too, and take a man who wasn't worth the time of day.

Back then, when I walked for so many days holding Lotte by the hand, when we drew strength from one another, I from her more than she from me, when we heard the women scream at night, and saw the dead hastily buried in roadside ditches in the morning so their bodies wouldn't be exposed to the midday sun – back then, not a word of complaint passed Lotte's lips. She said nothing when her shoes fell apart and she had to walk on with rags wrapped round her feet; when the carts were searched and looted; when the last of our possessions – our documents, clothes, food – were carried off. She said nothing and she didn't cry. But I cried, often, when she was asleep. I wasn't sad about the possessions we had lost. I was crying at Lotte's bravery.

Something happened on our journey.

The trek had to stop. For four days and four nights we moved neither forwards nor backwards. There was a fire somewhere way up ahead and they had to block the road. We waited. At night the countryside lay under the cold moonlight and the sound of the wind sweeping across the dry ground filled me with fear. I imagined I could see animals and figures creeping across the fields as soon as a cloud covered the moon. The earth we slept on was hard and cold, and Lotte's little body shivered beneath my coat. I'd seen that there was a farm a short distance from the road. It consisted of a farmhouse, a barn and some sheds. The tenant farmer lived there. People spoke badly of him. I'd seen him a number of times, with a big black dog on a leash, driving away people who were using his field as a latrine. But it was so cold. 'It'll be warm in the sheds,' I said, on the third night. 'We'll walk over there.' Lotte didn't want to. She said she didn't want to walk across the fields, the shadows between the furrows frightened her. I dismissed this. A roof over our heads and a bit of straw under our backs would do us good, I said.

We were still a long way off when we heard the dog bark. The farmer was standing on the doorstep. He was a heavy man with reddish hair and big, misshapen hands. He had on knee-length boots that were caked with earth. From behind him, inside the house, came the sound of a pot bubbling. I asked him if we could sleep in one of the sheds. He looked at us for a long time. There was nothing friendly in his eyes. But then he said yes, and I remember I laughed out loud and was instantly ashamed of my laughter.

The pigsty was empty. Perhaps he'd had to sell his pigs,

or had slaughtered them himself. We lay down on the straw. He gave us a few boiled potatoes and a horse blanket. We held the potatoes in our hands for a long time before eating them. They warmed us more than the blanket. Before I fell asleep I heard the animals rustling and chomping in the neighbouring shed, and just for a moment I thought it might all soon be over.

It must have been after midnight when the farmer came into the shed. The door opened almost soundlessly, but I wasn't sleeping deeply and I woke with a start. He came in and stopped in the middle of the room. The moon was at his back. His face was half in darkness and I couldn't make out his eyes, but I knew he was staring down at us. He was breathing heavily, and I could see his breath in the moonlight.

'Go away!' I whispered. 'Please, go!'

'I'd like to ask something of you,' he said.

'What, for heaven's sake?'

He took a step towards us, then stopped again. His face had now completely vanished into the darkness. His arm was slightly raised, and I gave a start, as I could see now that he had something in his hand. It was a dead chicken. He had grabbed it by the neck and the limp body was dangling from his fist.

'I'd like you to listen to me,' he said.

There was something sad in his voice, and I suddenly felt

sorry for him, standing there with the dead chicken in his hand. I said, 'Sit down. But be quiet; my little girl's asleep.'

He sat down beside us in the straw and started to talk. 'Maybe you'll understand me,' he said. 'I hope so. I really hope so. I know people like you. I know where you're from. And I know there's no going back. You . . . I saw you, you and your girl. Coming across the field towards the house. I saw you, and there was something . . . I don't know what it was, but I had a feeling you'd listen to me.' The farmer spoke slowly, haltingly, staring at the ground as if picking the words one by one out of the straw. 'I'm not old yet. But I can't sleep. At night the thoughts come. They're not nice thoughts. Sometimes I have the feeling they're not even mine. It's as if the thoughts come flying through the darkness across the fields and take root in me.' He raised his head and I saw his eyes; two tiny white moons were swimming in them. 'I had a woman once,' he went on. 'A good woman. She wanted to stay with me. We sat at the same table and slept in the same bed. I heard her breathing in the night. And the sound of her breathing drove the thoughts away.'

He fell silent. A jolt passed through his body, and I thought he was about to get up and leave the shed, but then he slumped over again and stared at the ground. 'You've seen the land,' he whispered. 'It's big. But it's not big enough to support everything. In the beginning it was different. On warm evenings we would sit in front of the house and gaze into the distance. But I would always look at her face as well. It was so beautiful with the evening sun on it. I couldn't help but love her.'

He stared for a while at the moon in the rectangle of the doorway. Then he continued. 'So the years passed, and everything could have been fine. But at some point she grew restless. She couldn't keep her hands still. There was something in her, a longing, I don't know . . . In any case she wanted . . . she wanted things.'

Suddenly he got to his feet. He was excited, breathing heavily, and I was afraid Lotte would wake up. I said, 'Sit down, go on.' He sat down again.

'I thought it would all sort itself out. Maybe I should've . . . I don't know. At any rate, she became dissatisfied. She didn't want to sit out in front of the house of an evening any more. She said the countryside was bleak and the sun hurt her eyes. She became hard and mean. And I became hard as well. Maybe I was unfair. But what was I supposed to do? I was terribly afraid she might leave. I told her we had to have patience, and trust. We simply had to stay together. That's what I kept telling her.'

The farmer bent forward. It looked as if he was in pain. Then he sat up straight again and went on talking. His voice was trembling now, and he was whispering even more quietly than before.

'One evening in spring I was sitting alone outside the

house. I'd been drinking, and the land stretched out in front of me as if it had no limits. Suddenly everything seemed easy again, and I wanted to show her all this beauty. I wanted to put my arms around her; I thought she would understand me, and from now on everything would be fine. I called her name, but she didn't answer, so I went into the house. She was sitting at the table, staring at a bowl of onions. I told her to come outside with me, I wanted to show her something. But she just shook her head, and that made me angry. I slammed the door behind me and started badgering her. I wanted her finally to understand, and I wanted things to go back to the way they were before. I raised my voice. I reproached her. I said terrible things. I shouted and raged. I slammed my fists against the kitchen cupboard. I took the bowl of onions and threw it at the plate rack. I stamped on the crockery and the onions. The shards cracked and crunched under my boots, and everything, everything went to pieces.'

He sat for a long time without moving. His eyes were closed and he was breathing deeply. Just as I thought he'd fallen asleep, he started speaking again.

'I'd like to ask something of you,' he said. 'It's just a little thing. I brought you the chicken. There are eggs and turnips in the house. Take as many as you can carry. Take all of them.'

'What do you want?' I asked.

'I want you to leave me alone for a moment with your

daughter. Just go out of the shed. Nothing will happen. You can trust me. You see, I think it's a gift. You found your way to me. And her presence is the gift I've waited for for so long.' The farmer grabbed my arm. 'Trust me,' he said. 'I'm not a bad man. Please, trust me.'

What can I say? We were hungry. And there was something so sad about him. I wasn't afraid that he might do something bad. And so I laid Lotte's head on the straw, covered her, and went outside.

The night was cold and still. The fields lay in the moonlight, and I could make out the line of carts in the distance, stretching beyond the horizon. The smell of burnt wood hung in the air. I thought I would boil the chicken and the turnips. The eggs I planned to wrap in my woollen scarf and keep. Perhaps I would pack them in straw. That would protect them from the sun.

Not a sound came from the shed. I'd left the door ajar, but I couldn't hear a thing. I thought of what the farmer had said: *her presence is a gift.* Another thought came to me, and for a few seconds I closed my eyes. I seemed to hear my heart beating. It was beating so loudly I thought surely it could be heard all around.

I crept back to the shed and peered through the gap in the door. It took a while for my eyes to grow accustomed to the dark. I saw the farmer's shapeless bulk. He was kneeling, motionless, beside Lotte in the straw. His hands lay open on his knees. He was leaning over her, gazing into her face. I barely had time to think how peaceful it looked, this image of the kneeling man and the sleeping child, when I saw that Lotte's eyes were open. In the shadow of his body I hadn't seen her face straight away. But now I saw that she was staring at the man, and I saw the horror in her eyes.

I pushed open the door and screamed. I pummelled his back with my fists, and out of the corner of my eye I saw him slump aside with a faint whimper as I grabbed Lotte and ran with her into the open. I lifted her up to my chest and only stopped running when we got to the road, where I crawled under a cart and covered her with my body as best I could.

And that was what I carried with me for the rest of my long journey: the image of my child's eyes like two bright drops of water in the darkness of the night.

The next day they opened the road and we moved on.

I spent so many interminable hours staring at our shadows on the ground in front of us that it seems to me they must still be travelling today, all alone, without us, on and on and on.

Heiner Joseph Landmann

Good morning.

What did you feel, citizens of Paulstadt, when you lowered me into this hole and Richard Regnier threw a bent hazel twig after me in farewell? What did you think when the priest gave his speech? He had to stand on a kitchen stool to make himself heard, because you all came – and for that I thank you. These are my final thanks, from the grave, which, by the way, is nothing like as uncomfortable as I always feared.

And what a lot of trouble the poor priest took with his speech! Not a word of it was true. Because truth is merely something for which we yearn.

Here I lie, your mayor, Heiner Joseph Landmann. My father, Heiner Joseph Landmann Snr., lies beside me, less than an arm's length away. We were never this close in life.

And his father in turn, my grandfather, Theodor C. Land-mann, lies about a metre and a half below us. You sink down over time.

Theodor C. was an architect and, as I'm sure you know, he designed the municipal park and the school building. He was good at calculation, and could draw trees better than anyone. He was also a philanthropist. Which Heiner Joseph Snr. definitely wasn't. He couldn't stand people. In fact, he hated most of them, including my mother and me. This was probably exactly why he became mayor and managed to hang on to the position for almost seventeen years. It created the distance he felt was necessary between himself and other people. He was a bad man and a bad father, and I was a stupid kid who wanted to do everything better than him. And, in a way, I succeeded.

I stuck it out even longer than you, Papa: twenty-nine years. That's how long the fate of this town was in my hands.

And if that doesn't sound good, then I don't know what good is.

And yet you all never tire of reproaching me for my mistakes. Even here, in the damp depths of my grave, your complaints filter through. You say I made unscrupulous promises I couldn't keep. But what else was I supposed to do? I was a politician. And I did try. I stood for office because I wanted something for the town. The best. Or at least: nothing bad. Something different from Papa, anyway.

You say I eliminated my competitors, one after another, by any means possible. Yes, that's exactly what I did. (Though not that many means were needed, incidentally.)

I hear you muttering about leaky ballot boxes. About voting slips that went missing and others that were counted two or three times. But, dear God, who asks the ram where he got his horns as long as he can lead the herd safely through the winter?

You say I overdid it with the women. To be honest, I don't know how it's possible to overdo it with women.

You talk about bribery. Bribery, you say, is a wicked thing. But I ask you, how could I have given without ever taking first? You can't dig deep into empty pockets.

At this precise moment one of you, one of the braver ones, no doubt, one of those who always knew, or at least maintains that he did, might step forward and ask, in a firm voice: Could you at least be more serious in death than you were in life, Landmann? My answer: No.

You say that I ripped off old Karl Jonas when I conned him out of his fields? That I greased the palms of the geological surveyors and the surveying engineers, then held out both hands when the construction contract for our leisure centre was awarded, the centre you all wanted so badly? My dear friends, far be it from me to call you liars! Yes, I did slightly speed up the process. The future was rattling at the gates of our town – I just happened to be standing there, and pocketed the entrance fee.

Later on, things happened over which I no longer had any control. If I'd had any control over them, they wouldn't have happened. You all remember the terrible day when three people lost their lives beneath the debris. Girders were wrongly placed, steel was hardened too early, concrete poured too late, the ground too soft, too deep, too undermined, I don't know.

The deaths of these three people were a disaster for us all. Their graves are over there, plot seven, rows four and five.

Stephan Wichant. Friedbert Loheim. Martha Avenieu.

Do you know what was the most poignant moment of my life? Not my appointment as mayor, nor my first kiss from the girl who would later become my wife (you know how that ended). Not even the birth of my first child, which back then I still took for granted. No: it was the moment when we all gathered together in plot seven, rows four and five, to send three of our fellow citizens off on their final journey.

At that moment our hearts all beat together, as if we were a single organism. For that one, desperately sad moment we were what people call a *community*.

*

Family is the closest community of all. Who would contradict me on that? No one. So I'll have to do it myself. Family is just a community of necessity. That can work out, but often doesn't. We just don't know what faces we'll be looking at when we leave the familiar universe of the womb. A community like the one that came together that autumn Saturday afternoon is something else entirely. It arose out of the free will of each individual member.

And that is what I mean.

As you know, my mother left us right after releasing me into the world. In those days cancer still often went undiagnosed, and, as a fervent Catholic, Mama thought the Devil was living inside her and taking a piece of her liver every day. For as long as she could still speak, she cursed the doctors, refused to take her medicine, and instead consigned her soul to the wooden Jesus on the wall of her sickroom. I think she was a very unsophisticated woman.

Legend has it that, at the age of four, I said: I'm going to be mayor, and there's nothing you can do about it! I've no idea whether I was really able to grasp the meaning of my words; in any case, it seems I stamped my feet one after the other on the living-room floorboards. I was a stubborn little mule; I probably thought that, as mayor, you'd always have enough grown-up women around you, and also that nothing bad could happen to you ever again. The first part of this assumption is correct, the second is not.

Cancer got me, too.

Do you know Friedrich Sertürner? Friedrich Wilhelm Adam Sertürner would have liked to become an architect, but he became a pharmacist instead. And that was a stroke of luck for me. Because in the year 1804 (when the population of Paulstadt still consisted of just four farming families, all related but all sworn enemies, their farms centred on a marshy pool more or less where Kobielski's car dump is today), Sertürner got hold of a few spoonfuls of pure opium from somewhere and distilled it to make a poppy alkaloid. He named it morphium, after Morpheus, the Greek god of dreams, son of Hypnos, shapeshifter, messenger between the worlds, and the god of peaceful death into the bargain, which definitely makes him a congenial figure in my view.

You can sort of understand Mama: cancer is a devilish business. You can carry it around with you for years and not notice a thing, then all of a sudden it kicks off. It's early morning, you're sitting on the toilet with the local newspaper, about to look at the readers' letters, and suddenly you feel this pain. It's as if a dog has sunk its teeth into your kidneys and is tearing them out of your body piece by piece. Not just any old dog; one with bloodshot eyes, hulking, stupid and mean. You press both fists to your belly, fall sideways off the toilet and writhe on the tiles. Someone calls your name, hammers on the door, breaks it down: screams, paramedic, blue light, hospital, etc.

With the first injection you already feel better, and later, when you're hooked up to a drip and the pain gradually fades to a vague memory as you contemplate the infinite beauty of the ceiling light over your bed, you feel as if everything will be all right again.

It won't, of course. Your body starts to decay and crumble like an old wooden barrel. But in the end it was quick, and relatively pleasant. Morpheus cradled me into death.

I remember that once, as a kid, I shat on the compost heap, which Papa then turned over with his pitchfork. Today, more or less on the spot where the compost heap used to be, there stands the glass office block of the Lainsam & Sons insurance company. That says quite a bit about the transience of all that is human.

I remember an old pot I found in a corner of our cellar. I peed in it and used it to fertilize the tomato plants in the garden. Later I found out that the pot wasn't a pot but Grandfather's steel helmet, which had a piece missing. It was shot away by a sharp-eyed Englishman, along with a large part of Grandfather's left temple. He lived another forty-six years after that, and did pretty well on the whole.

I remember the many hands I've shaken, and the few hands that have held me.

I remember the sun on the snow-covered fields. It had only just risen, and a few larks shot up into the sky as if fleeing its cold light.

I remember my father.

I remember my armchair in the town hall. I'd inherited it from my aunt, and my first act of officialdom was to have it lugged up to the mayoral office. It had woodworm; wood flour trickled from one leg, and horsehair bulged out of rips in the upholstery. It was old, ugly and not especially comfortable. But it belonged to me and me alone. It felt like a tiny piece of native habitat amid all the craziness around me. I could sit down in it, lean back, bury my hands in the horsehair, and feel as if I had something like a home.

And with that, dear people of Paulstadt, let's return for the last, the very last, time to my failings. Yes, I bribed people, I made false promises, and probably a whole heap of illegitimate children as well; I lied and cheated, I was bad, I was wicked, I was deceitful and mean. To summarize: friends, I was one of you!

Oh yes – one more thing. Some young people have been picnicking on our grave lately on mild summer evenings, among them old Schwitters' son, an utter idiot with no decency or manners. They picked this grave because it's got a huge slab of black Labrador marble that retains the heat of the sun until well after nightfall. There they sit, yattering non-stop, the most egregious nonsense, spilling their beer, which trickles over our family name engraved in the marble and makes the letters sticky. Sometimes young Schwitters pees against the back of the gravestone, and the girls all giggle and shriek. I resent them for it. I hate them for their stupidity and their beauty. I hate them for the miracle inside them, on which they waste not a single thought behind their hot, unwrinkled foreheads.

Can someone go and ask them to stay for ever?

Martha Avenieu

As a girl, I used to write long letters to imaginary men. I would perfume the silk paper pages, slip them into unstamped envelopes and drop them, with thumping heart, into the post box. I wonder if they were ever opened.

Later I wrote a novel, but no one wanted to read it to the end. I burned the pile of pages out in the middle of the fields. They were almost completely burnt when the wind blew on the ashes, and I stood there in a flurry of fluttering shadows as if in a swarm of dainty black butterflies.

I wasn't like the other girls. I lacked their propensity for cheerfulness, and sometimes I despaired of my dreams. I felt all wrong in my body, with its thin arms and long neck, as wrong as I did in this town with its bumpy roads and the smell of mould that escaped from cellar windows in summer. At night, I lay in bed with the window open, hugging a pillow tight against my breast, yearning for freedom and light.

A few days before my nineteenth birthday I met Robert.

He was sitting on a bench in the town hall square, and I thought he looked lost somehow. His jacket was buttoned up wrong, and when I saw his small hands resting in his lap I felt a warmth in me that I'd never known before. When our eyes met, we didn't smile. Right from the start we were connected in some strange way. We were so different, our thoughts and feelings running in opposite directions, yet we belonged together. We were two diverging branches on the trunk of the same tree.

We married before we even turned twenty. Robert's proposal was clumsy. He dropped the ring and had to crawl after it, right under the kitchen bench. His shirt rode up out of his trousers until I could see his boyish white back. I think we both laughed. Then I took the ring and said yes. It was a wonderful party. I danced all night and drank wine and enjoyed myself. Through my veil the wedding guests' faces looked soft and beautiful, and for the first time in my life I felt like a woman.

Back then, the town was slowly starting to wake up. Hot tar steamed on every corner, whole rows of houses were being renovated, and Marktstrasse acquired wide pavements equipped with streetlamps. On the evening of my twenty-first birthday I was standing under one of those streetlamps with Robert, talking to him urgently. Excited by my own determination and by the wine we'd been drinking, I stopped and seized his hands as we were walking home. 'I want to make something of our life,' I said. 'I want to do something, to work and grow. I want to open a business. With you.'

I could see him trying to look composed, but I also saw that the veins at his temple were bulging like roots, and pulsating as if they might burst at any minute. 'What sort of business do you mean?' he asked.

'I mean a shop, for shoes. An upmarket shoe shop. We don't have anything like that yet in Paulstadt; people go off God knows where to buy shoes. I have a little money. Our parents can help. We'll pool our savings. The coal merchant's on the ground floor has been empty for years. Just think: the two of us, you and me, in our own little shoe shop! You'll see – all we need is a little courage. Would you like that, Robert? Would you like to be courageous with me?'

His face crumpled slightly; but then he said, 'Well, we should do something, of course. Get to grips with something. And maybe it isn't such a bad idea.'

I flung my arms around his neck and kissed him.

The business took off. Word soon got around that a new shoe shop had opened on the outskirts of town, and the little bell that Robert had managed, after a few failed attempts, to fix above the door rang at almost all hours of the day. The house was on the approach road, near the main road heading west. Our apartment was right above the shop; at dawn I could see the commuters' faces behind their windscreens, and if I leaned out of the window I could wipe the dust off the sign that read *Martha's Quality Ladies' Shoes*. I worked from eight in the morning till six in the evening; I checked the stock, displayed the merchandise and attended to our clients' wishes. Robert was responsible for the bookkeeping, and sometimes the two of us would sit up all night at the kitchen table trying to insert some order into his muddled system.

Robert was a man full of insecurities and anxieties, and it was an effort for him to hold his own in life, which he saw as a perpetual challenge. He was always fighting the worries that plagued him and the objects that seemed to stand in the way of his fidgety limbs.

The bungled marriage proposal was just the first in a long series of clumsinesses. Shoeboxes and tins of polish slipped from his hands; shoe trees, brushes, open cash boxes all fell to the floor, and almost every week documents and receipts went missing. He didn't know how to treat objects. And he didn't know how to treat a woman. It was as if Robert's hands were leading a life of their own, incapable of expressing his ideas about love.

One night I asked him, 'What do you really desire, Robert?'

'How do you mean?'

'I mean in bed.'

'Oh,' was all he said.

'Tell me,' I insisted.

'I don't think I have any desires in that regard,' he said.

I would have liked to have had a child. I often imagined what it would be like to cradle a little person like that in my arms. When they got bigger, I'd take them by the hand and walk with them across the fields. We'd weave ourselves crowns of field flowers and spin round and round in the white drifts beneath the poplars.

Sometimes, at night, when another month had gone by, I would listen to Robert breathing beside me, feel his body twitch in sleep, and tremble with happiness and longing for what was to come.

But it didn't happen. It's pointless looking for reasons; there's no explanation and no blame. I didn't reproach Robert, and instead of succumbing to despair I put all my energy into running the business. I wanted to move out of our road, which I found increasingly grey and dreary, into the centre of town, and I started looking for suitable premises. I dreamed of a splendid showroom, light and spacious, and shop assistants whose elegance was on a par with that of their customers. Every night I imagined what it would be like to create an atmosphere like this, full of life and light. Sometimes I would creep down the dark stairs and try on one of the latest models. I would walk around the shop, observe myself in the mirror, and smile as I never did when I was a young girl.

Our troubles began with the death of the florist, Greg-orina Stavac. They found the body of the poor woman, whom hardly anyone in Paulstadt had really known, in the back room of her shop on Marktstrasse. The location of the shop was ideal, but the price was more than we could afford. Less than two months after the funeral, a big, modern shoe shop opened in its place. The owner was Edward Millborg, a thickset man with a grey beard and watery blue eyes. He described himself as an entrepreneur and was in various lines of business, for which his friendship with the mayor was an advantage. Whatever the weather, he always wore a straw hat and a pale suit with a collar that was covered in stains from all the pomade in his hair.

'He'll have it easy, with all his money and the good loca-tion,' said Robert, and I felt a wave of hatred surge inside me.

'Shut up,' I said. 'Just shut up!'

Every Friday morning, Edward Millborg went to his shop to check on things and pay the assistants their wages. He would sit in the cashier's chair, handing out wage packets and little chocolates wrapped in silver paper, and laughing non-stop.

On one such Friday I went to Marktstrasse to speak to him. There were various things I wanted to say. They were things of the greatest importance, which had been very clear in my mind the previous night. But when I saw him sitting in the midst of all those women, I couldn't remember a single one. Edward Millborg sat there with his hat pushed back on his head and popped a sweet into his mouth.

'I'd like to talk to you,' I said.

He looked at me and said, 'Who are you, madam?' He said it with a smile, but there was no mockery in it.

The women retreated and busied themselves at the shelves.

'I think you know very well who I am,' I said. 'My name is Martha Avenieu.'

He continued to smile as he shifted the sweet from one cheek to the other. Suddenly he got to his feet and held out his hand. 'What can I do for you, madam?'

I looked around. The space seemed much bigger than it appeared from outside. Millborg had clearly knocked down the dividing wall to the back room.

'It must have been over there that they found her,' I said.

'Who?' he asked.

'The florist. About there, more or less, next to the shelf with the Italian men's shoes.'

'Oh,' said Edward Millborg. He raised his hat for a moment and ran his hand quickly over his hair, which gleamed in the light from the little overhead lamps.

'Nobody noticed a thing,' I said, a bit louder than I'd intended. 'There was no one who missed her, you see?'

The saleswomen had stopped what they were doing. Tissue paper rustled in a shoebox.

'All her life she was alone,' I continued. 'I don't think anyone really saw her.'

Edward Millborg stood motionless. He wasn't smiling any more. I wanted to keep talking, I wanted to hurl things right in his face, but I didn't know what to say.

'You think you've got it easy, with all your money and this good location,' I shouted. 'But you don't understand the first thing about shoes, you stupid man. You poor, stupid, horrible man!'

The cold February wind hit me as I stepped out onto the street. The ice in the gaps between the paving stones was black with the dirt of the long winter. Only a few people were out on the pavement. They walked bent forward, their faces hidden in thick scarves. On the other side of the street Margarete Lichtlein was pulling her handcart along behind her and talking into the rain that was starting to fall.

In the shop Robert was sitting behind the cash desk filing papers. He had a separate folder for each procedure, labelled in different colours: outgoings, receipts, orders, complaints. Robert loved his coloured folders.

'How did it go?' he asked. 'Did you do it?'

His face was full of childlike anticipation, and I could have punched it. I was furious with this man whose small, clean hands didn't know how to touch anything other than folders and lay still and useless on the blanket every night.

'I . . . I think,' I started; but then I lost control. 'Yes, I did it! And I'm going to do more. A woman should have much more still to do in her life, don't you agree?'

In a few quick moves I snatched up the folders from the cash desk and ran out of the door. The wind was even stronger now, whipping the rain down the road. I didn't throw the folders in the air, or fling them as hard as I could across the pavement. I just let them fall. I watched the colours of Robert's handwriting blur in the dirty grey of the puddles. I saw him through the rain streaming down the shop window, and I saw the horror in his face.

That night in bed we lay beside each other and I heard him weeping in the dark. Presumably he had both hands over his face and was sobbing into his palms. Before this, I had often wanted to hold him, weeping, in my arms. I'd imagined that tears would establish a wordless understanding between us. But now all I felt was disgust. Here in my bed lay not a man but a little child, and it was making a mess of our freshly washed pillowcases.

The day it happened, we were alone in the shop at around noon. The sun was shining through the front window in flickering shafts of light, settling on display models coated in a fine layer of dust. Apart from the fountain pen in Robert's hand scratching across the pages of a new folder, it was quiet. I was perched on a fitting stool, sticking price labels on sandals. The shop smelled of leather. I'd never been so conscious of the smell. Everything was steeped in it. Even the silence smelled of leather. Robert was writing. His gestures were calm and absolutely even; they were steeped in boredom and monotony, along with everything else. I leaped up from my stool.

'Let's go!' I said. 'We're going out. Somewhere we can be free and can let our thoughts fly.'

'What about the shop?' asked Robert, behind the cash desk.

'The shop's closed today.'

We drove around for a while in our car. It was a warm, sunny day with only the occasional shadow of a cloud moving across the fields. I opened the window and breathed in the scent of summer. In the distance the domed roof of the Paulstadt leisure centre flashed in the sun, and suddenly my sense of expectation was mingled with a longing for people, for the sound of their voices, for laughter and music.

We stopped in the car park, a vast, blindingly bright expanse of concrete with only a few cars dotted about here and there. When I got out of the car and stepped into the sunlight, the thought occurred to me that my life so far had been nothing but a strange misunderstanding, and I felt so happy and free that I would have liked to kick the shoes off my feet and dance on the hot concrete.

Robert didn't want to come. He said he'd rather stay in the car and wait for me. I felt a surge of anger, but then I saw those small, nervous hands in his lap and the anger subsided again. I took his face in my hands and kissed him on the forehead. I hadn't done anything like that for a long time. His skin was damp and warm, and I kissed him as one kisses a child, in farewell, or to comfort.

When I entered the building I was surprised by the cool air, which was a surreal contrast to the heat of the car park. Everything was spacious and bright. The walls and marble floors sparkled, and columns of light beamed down through the high glass roof. A young sales assistant was standing behind a display window, looking out in my direction. She just looked at me, and I walked on, past the restaurant with the palm trees in big tubs, the ice-cream parlour with the little porcelain figures on all the tables, the fountain lit up all the colours of the rainbow, the bowling alley and the betting shop, the amusement arcade full of ringing, beeping, humming slot machines.

A man walked past, gazing upwards. He stopped and shielded his eyes with his hands. I saw his shoulders tense. Then he lowered his hands and backed away. He retreated slowly, his face still turned towards the ceiling. I don't know why I didn't follow his gaze. I think I was wondering what it would be like to embrace this man, and perhaps I might even have done it, but at that moment he suddenly turned and started running. Then I heard the sound, a hoarse screech swiftly rising to a crescendo. It was as if the air were vibrating, creating this all-pervasive screech all by itself. I felt a tremor beneath my feet. Then I saw the ground move. I saw the man stumble and fall, an expression of furious astonishment on his face. He stumbled because the ground opened up in front of him, and he fell down and put his hands over his head, and I saw that his hands were covered in blood. I heard a woman scream. But her voice was swallowed up by the screeching air and the creaking of fake marble that burst like ice on the surface of water that has begun to flow. Out of the corner of my eye I saw someone run past, bent double, jacket pulled over their head for protection. Perhaps I would have made it if I'd run after them, but for some reason I was rooted to the spot. Now I saw the woman. She was lying by the wreckage of a stone slab that had fallen off the wall. She was hugging her knees to her chest and her face, too, was turned upwards. Her mouth was forming words I didn't understand. I looked up. And I saw the glass dome burst apart with a single, muffled report. It was as if, in a brief moment of true beauty, the heavens split and opened themselves to the light.

But isn't it strange that, at that very moment, as I gazed up at the fine, glittering rain of glass splinters that sliced into my face a second later, I had a vision? It was a clear picture of my husband Robert, who was sitting outside in the parked car with his hands in his lap, hands that would achieve nothing else ever again for the whole of the rest of his life.

Robert Avenieu

At night, when she crept downstairs again to pose in front of the mirror and enjoy feeling like some sort of French tart, I didn't stay in bed: I sat at the open window where I could look out onto the road and breathe freely at last. It was quiet, the only sound the occasional swish of car tyres; the roofs projected their outline onto the night sky, and there was a smell of old, damp walls, especially in spring, after the first warm rain.

When I was a child, my mother often urged me never to regret anything. She said regret didn't alter what had happened, it just weighed on the soul, and there was no sense or point to it, anyway. She was right, of course, but I wasn't like her. I usually regretted things even as I was doing them, which didn't exactly make life easier.

I first saw Martha in the town hall square. She was walking back and forth with two girlfriends, laughing constantly. I was sitting on a bench, and every time she walked past she turned her head towards the town hall and seemed to be gazing at the tower, or the clock, or something in that direction. I'd already noticed her incredibly long neck. It was long and slender and it drove me crazy. I didn't know what I was supposed to do; I just sat there on the bench, feeling every bit as stupid as I probably was.

I found out where she lived, and one day I stood outside and waited until she came out of the house. She didn't look at me at first, just walked straight past. Then she turned and said, 'You think you're quite the daredevil, don't you?'

'No,' I said. 'Not at all.'

'Things can't move fast enough for you.'

I stared at her neck. 'Don't know,' I said.

'Well, you can't be expected to know everything,' she said. 'But there's no harm in making an effort, is there?'

'No,' I said. 'Sure.'

'So what shall we do now?'

'No idea,' I said. 'Walk around the block, maybe?'

'Such a daredevil,' she said, and off we went.

We were married soon afterwards. I proposed to her, and as I tried to put the ring on her finger she stared straight at me the whole time. Her eyes seemed to bore into mine, and I started to have doubts. The ring fell out of my hand and rolled under the kitchen bench. She burst into peals of laughter, and at that moment I sensed that this might be the start of a colossal misunderstanding.

She was always talking about love. For me, love was neither a blessing from God nor the result of some sort of effort; it was just a word like any other. Martha had interested me because I was lonely, and because you had to have a girl. And I married her because I wanted children. Although I was young, there was hardly anything else I wanted from life.

I'd set my heart on making a cradle myself, with my own hands. With wooden rockers and silken drapes. I imagined what it would be like to hear the sounds that little person made in the darkness of our bedroom. Martha said I was bound to saw off my fingers. She saw us as two diverging branches on the trunk of the same tree. But that's not the case. We had no roots in common. I'm not even sure we breathed the same air. We stood beside each other for years among racks of shoes that held no interest for me; we slept in the same bed, ate at the same table, looked out of the same window onto the same approach road. We spent half our lives in the same room without ever really touching each other.

'I'd like to have a child,' I said to Martha. 'People need to extend beyond themselves.'

'Let me think about it,' she said. 'Something like that needs careful consideration. And we've got time, anyway, haven't we?'

She always said things like that. Words that were supposed to fill the emptiness between us but had no meaning whatsoever.

Then she got pregnant. It was like a miracle that neither of us could really comprehend.

Why don't you sit down, the nurse says, this may take a while. I shake my head and go over to the window. A man is standing under a tree, poking a stick into a pile of leaves. A young boy runs past him, laughing. The man pauses and just stands there, stick in one hand, the other buried in his trouser pocket. The branches above him sway in the wind. Suddenly it all happens very fast. She screams. Her voice sounds strange. She throws her head back and digs her fingers into the mattress. The midwife is working with both hands. Her shoulders rise and fall. Quick, she says, and the nurse runs out of the room. You're doing well, says the midwife, you're doing really well, just keep going. Oh God, she groans, oh God, oh God, oh God. I touch her sheet. Can I maybe, I say, and don't know how to go on. She groans again, a long-drawn-out wail, rising and falling. My hand rests on the sheet like a lump of wood. The nurse comes back. There's a doctor with her. He doesn't say anything, just lets the nurse help him into the gloves, then goes over to the bed. Suddenly it's hot in the room. The doctor and the midwife work shoulder to shoulder in silence. The midwife strokes her thumb across my wife's cheek and whispers something in her ear. She touches her face as if that were completely natural, and probably it is. This might get unpleasant now, the doctor tells me, but you don't have to stay. I try to meet her eyes. She closes them. Quick, he says, and rolls up his sleeves. The nurse grabs my shoulders and pushes me out of the room. This is no place for men, she says, only doctors. She laughs and disappears again. There's a couple sitting in the waiting area. They're holding each other's hands and looking at me. I go to the toilet and wash my face. I look in the mirror and feel ashamed. For a moment I can't believe that this is me. I come out of the toilet. The couple have gone. I sit down, listen to the sounds and the screams coming from the room, and wait. Then it goes quiet. Nothing happens for a long time. Finally the door opens and the midwife is standing there. I'm so sorry, she says, but she didn't need to say it. Later, she puts her hand on my arm. Do you want to see him? Yes, I say. He's lying on a lime-green pillow. His arms are stretched out to the sides. His face is tiny. There's a streak of yellow slime on his temple. His eyes are hidden between deep folds of skin. I pick up the pillow for a moment. It's much lighter than I expected. I look over at her. A thin strand of hair is stuck to her cheek, and a patch of sunlight trembles on her brow. She turns her head and looks out of the window.

I didn't reproach her. I didn't pester her. I didn't pity her. In any case, she soon seemed to have forgotten the matter. 'Yesterday's dreams fade,' she said once, 'but every night brings a new dream, isn't that wonderful?' When I heard her say that, I realized that I hated her. I hated everything about her: her voice, her face, her smile, and most of all I hated her neck, that long, thin caricature of a neck. I stroked her hair and said, 'Yes, dear, it's wonderful.'

She always said I didn't understand anything about beauty. But that's not true. I just didn't understand anything about the things she understood to be beautiful. I hadn't got a clue about poetry, but when she let me read one of her poems I knew straight away it was no good. It was about a woman on a journey, a fearful creature sitting on a train in a sequinned dress and white shoes and feeling exposed to the gaze of strange men. It had no rhythm, no melody and no soul, just a few distorted and overblown images. A sequinned dress, on a train!

In the nights when Martha was downstairs parading in front of the mirror, I would sit at the window and imagine what things would have been like without her. I tried to picture myself somewhere, as far away as possible, somewhere without tired commuters' faces, without dusty shelves and the smell of leather, without the customers' stupid questions, without this woman's dreams that were not mine. I would sit there staring out into the night until I heard her footsteps on the stairs, when I would creep back into bed and pretend to be asleep.

'Let's go,' she cried that day. 'We're going out!' She jumped up from the fitting stool as if she'd been stung. Her face was flushed, she was so taken by her idea. I had no objections. The shop hadn't been doing well for a long time by then. To tell the truth, it was completely dead.

We drove to the new leisure centre with the glass roof that glittered above the fields in the distance. 'I have such a longing in me,' she cried. 'I want to be among people! I want to feel their warmth and hear their laughter!' She was shouting stuff like that across the concrete expanse of the car park, where a few vehicles sat glowing in the heat.

I said, 'Go by yourself. I don't feel like it.'

'Of course you're coming,' she said.

'No,' I said.

There was a flash of malice in her eyes. For a moment I thought she was going to slap me.

'You're my husband, aren't you?' she asked.

'Yes,' I said.

She nodded, took a step away from the car, then immediately turned again and I thought: this is it. But then something unexpected happened. She took my face in her hands and kissed my forehead. Her lips were cool and dry. I felt like a fool. She walked away, then stopped again. For a moment she stood there in the sunlight, arms slightly raised, as if talking to some invisible person, or as if she were a little girl again, about to start dancing. Then she vanished in the shadow of the entrance.

The heat pressed through the open window into the car. I moved to sit behind the wheel, started the engine and drove slowly out of the car park. When I got to the main road I put my foot down. It was nice to feel the wind. It blew in among some loose papers I'd forgotten in a folder on the back seat; the pages whirled about behind me. I turned on the radio. I didn't know what the music was, but it was good. In the rear-view mirror I saw the glass roof vanish beneath the undulating horizon. I wasn't thinking about her any more. Perhaps I was thinking about the road that was simply there, laid out across the landscape in front of me, or the steering wheel, which was vibrating and felt a little sticky. Really, though, I wasn't thinking about anything any more.

Sophie Breyer

Idiots.

Heribert Kraus

Early morning. The road is wet. Drops are falling from the trees; underneath them it already smells of autumn. The light, as if someone had poured it over the roofs. Now it's running down them, down chimneys, gutters, walls, like viscous gold. The pigeons' cooing and fluttering sounds unfamiliar. It's too early to think clearly. Don't think, keep pedalling, it's a long round! And your legs are still stiff. It's cold. The bike is heavy. Steel – has to withstand a lot. Full bags. And cobbles everywhere. An old town. Old houses. Old streets. Good for the townscape, bad for postmen. Keep pedalling, it'll get easier soon. It's just the beginning that's hard. The beginning and the end.

Turning off Leinestrasse into Thomasstrasse, on into the day. Windows flash. The sky so bright it hurts your eyes. Across Kernerplatz, past the oldest tree. The hollow trunk, just wide enough for three children to hide in. The dahlias. The grass. The hole in the ground. A fox, perhaps. Probably nothing left to eat out there in the fields. The nursery school. Wonky animal drawings on the wall. Giraffe. Elephant. Tiger. The hippopotamus is squinting; dew glitters on the bars of the swing. A cap on the grass like a yellow flower.

Karolinenstrasse. Kornweg. Brückenstrasse. The delivery starts at number three. There's no numbers one and two. No one knows why.

And how's the little girl? asks Frau Haller, at the fence. Wizened face, but always friendly. Plucks at her dressing gown. Always the same dressing gown, never a different one. Over the years I've watched it fade, its rich, bright red dwindling to pallid, salmony pink. And what do the doctors say? No one ever wishes for such a thing, of course. But what can you do? Mine left long ago. Womb, home, everything, that's just the way it is. But yours is still small. It must be hard. Oh – heading off already? By all means. Have a nice day. See you tomorrow. See you tomorrow!

Brückenstrasse is one of the best. All old people, not much post. The air is already warm. The road stretches ahead in the sun; tarred only recently, and it split again immediately afterwards. Dark cracks. Holes. Troughs. The town has no money. No one has money; but at least it smells of coffee. Of bread and sausage and honey and chocolate. Of bacon and fat-fried eggs. Of toilet odours and soap suds. Through the open windows, past the laundry, houses exhale the remnants of the night. Shaken-out dreams lie in the grass below. Who said that? You? Well, who'd have thought. In the distance, Frau Heller is still standing at the garden fence, a salmon-pink blob, waving.

Conversations are to be avoided at all costs. Other people's loneliness is not yours. That's what Walther used to say. Forty-seven years in the postal service and only off sick once. Renal colic. Two days in bed with compresses and thistle tea, then back on his bike again. Later, he showed the youngsters the rounds. Oversaw the expansion to two postal districts, then four. Four neighbourhoods, four postmen, one stand-in. If you've got a problem, ask Walther. He'll know. If he doesn't know, it means there isn't a problem. Then one day, his heart. Keeled over on his way to the office, right outside Dürrstrasse 7, the house with the foreign travel brochures.

Leberstrasse. Greinerplatz. The Golden Moon stands in its own shadow, as if it swallows the sunlight. In front, on the pavement, a half-empty wine glass with a cigarette butt. Three or four people still inside. The landlord lives at the back of the pub and refuses to give up.

Turning off Greinerplatz into Halbgasse. Gleimstrasse. Wernerstrasse. New houses on old foundations, like crowns on broken teeth. The blind windows of number seven. Never a soul to be seen, yet still the letters keep coming, small envelopes with pale blue handwriting. In front, the big construction pit where an excavator has lain for years, sunk, rusting, bucket pointed at the sky. No excavator holds its bucket up high after the end of the working day. This one does. The cherry tree outside number nine, and, barely discernible in the cherry tree's shadow: Herr Rudolf. Sitting there, mottled hands in his lap, eyes swollen and red. It's nice out here. Fresh air; can't complain. This tree's an old cripple, but it still has the juiciest cherries. Almost black already, and hardly any maggots. Want some? There's the basket. Need eating before the pests get them. We can't keep anything that grows, can we?

And, time and again, children. Seated in rooms. Staring behind curtains. Crawling through grass. They sit up, haul themselves to their feet, slip, fall, scream, cry, laugh, do it again and again. They can. They're healthy, and don't know how lucky they are. Sometimes, in a pushchair, a tiny crimson face. A foot, so small you can hardly believe it. And the big kids. Standing around smoking. You remember now: you did, too, exactly there. On the wall. Behind the hedge. On the bench in the bus shelter. Childhood is the place of first times. Keep going. It's got warm. Hot, actually. But not unpleasant. The wind in your face. It comes from far across the fields, bringing the smell of burnt straw. Another memory. Push it away. My child. Don't think about it. My child. Keep going. Down Mollardweg into Grünstrasse, seven envelopes and no brochures, round the corner, and then, finally: Marktstrasse. Pulsating artery, always throbbing with life, that's what it says in the publicity brochures on display at the town hall. The face of the town. Or its heart. Its pride and joy, at any rate. But it's just a street, really, no more than four hundred metres long. The lorries have to mount the pavement in order to squeeze past each other. It's true, though: always something going on. Over there, Yılmaz the men's tailor emerges from the cave of his shop, yawns and stretches, then totters half-blind into the sunlight, so thin he barely casts a shadow. Makes trousers and suits and brews Turkish tea. Strongest tea in the world, he says, and laughs: even the dead jump up and start dancing! Now he totters over to Lehmkuhl's. Oldest building on the square. Tables on the pavement, lunch for four euros fifty including a drink. Yılmaz needs to watch out that car doesn't hit him, or the bike right behind it. The cyclist is a teacher. Typical. What's a bell for? Probably preoccupied. Probably maths. Head full of numbers, and on his way home already at midday. On the other hand, better a bike than a tram. They were going to put one of those in here as well. Didn't come to anything. And, of course, thank God for that. Who needs a tram, for heaven's sake? In a town where you can walk from north to south in twenty-five minutes, west to east in less than twenty? No free tables in the Pastry Cook. All full of old ladies. The very finest cakes, but unhealthy, of course. Anything enjoyable is unhealthy. The whole of life is one long health risk from beginning to end. The ladies don't care. They sit there with their slices of cake, all done up, dressed to the nines, for what or for whom no one knows. Most of their husbands were laid to rest in the field long ago. Hardly any left. Now it's their own memory the ladies are preserving. Blouses, cardigans, silk scarves. Handbags the size of suitcases. Faces concreted with make-up, white, blue, violet hair whipped up like candy floss and topped with a hat, a scarf, a beret, pinned, tied, hooked, knotted. On the other side of the street Buxter the butcher is shutting up shop. Bloody apron, bloody hands, tired face. A bull of a man, but his shoulders nothing like as broad and round as they used to be. Just shutting up shop, at this time of day. Perhaps he doesn't need the custom. Or there's no more meat. Or no customers. One hears things. A man comes out of the Black Buck. Briefcase, suit, hat, in this heat. Over to Stranzl's bakery. Coffee, a bread roll to go, with butter, sausage, gherkins, and slices of egg so thin the green shimmers through the yolk. Or in it. You wouldn't have had that in the old days: cold meats at the bakery. The man in the hat likes it. Probably couldn't get breakfast at the Black Buck, or declined it, did some work on the frayed sofa in the foyer instead, or watched television in his room, now hurrying on, by car or bus, the bread roll on his lap and egg crumbs everywhere. Clanging and hammering from Tessler's ironmonger's. But the neighbours can complain as much as they like; police reports won't make any difference, nor will petitions to the town hall. Because old Tessler sits on the town council, and so does his daughter. This constant clanging and hammering all afternoon; sheet metal, supposedly. But why so many sheets of metal? Perhaps you don't hear it in Wittmann's wine bar across the road. Good wines. From Spain. The sun shines at you out of every glass, says Frau Wittmann, even in winter. Though there's nothing sunny about her at all. Her face is as white as a sheet. Applied umpteen times for a licence for tables outdoors. But the town hall won't budge: coffee and beer yes, wine no. Salaam aleikum! That's what you say, isn't it? The greengrocer. A true Paulstadter. You've got to hand it to him. Greets every passer-by, and tips the postman. The vegetables always fresh, like a painting. Something's going on at the police station. A man comes out. Looks around. Puts his hands on his hips. Used to be a terrible hooligan, now a policeman. Crosses over to Sophie Breyer's tobacconist's; copy of the local paper and chewing gum for the kids. Doesn't pay. Frau Breyer just laughs. And back to the police station; nothing else to do. The occasional fight. Very rarely, someone runs out on a bill. Once there was a suspected murder, but it was reduced to manslaughter. There was a letterbox fire recently, though. Flap pulled open. Wall covered in soot, blackened all the way to the ceiling. No other incidents. You can rest in peace in Paulstadt. For ever, ultimately. There was another recently. Old Frau

Kern, Hermstrasse 5, blue front door, only ever got letters from her grandson. Just nodded off in her armchair, plate of pickled gherkins in her lap. Or that kid in the marsh. Nothing to be done about it. We start dying the moment we first think about death. Listen – it's quiet! Tessler's are taking a break. Sitting there eating their sandwiches while the sheet metal cools down. And the swallows are already circling above the town hall. But why's the florist's closed? Not even a sign on the door. No flowers today. Well then, slide the brochures under the door. A cool draught from inside blows over the fingers. Gregorina. Her very name a promise. Try to picture the florist. Her figure. Her hair. Her face. They say it's faces that stay with you. But that's not true. None of them stay with you. Not even your own. Especially not your own.

In Weingasse it's quiet again. An alley so narrow the sun hardly ever finds its way in. Tiredness setting in now. Deep breaths. Sit down. On the steps of number nine. Thermos flask in side pocket, tea in winter, juice in summer. Biscuits in every season. The first pigeon is already pattering about in front of you. The stone is cool, it smells of dusty cellars and olden days. Don't think about it. Don't think about home. The upstairs room. The curtains, the bed, the blankets and pillows. The small face that seems always to be getting smaller. Completely white, whiter than the blankets and the pillows and the towels, freshly washed and piled up alongside. The little hand. As light as paper. Come on, get up! A biscuit for the pigeon, then you've got to keep going. Only four more streets. But it gets harder towards the end. Stabbing pain in the knees, and a trapped nerve in the shoulder. The doctor says it'll get better, but he doesn't have a clue. The doctors don't know anything. Or perhaps they know everything and are just comforting you, and that's the worst. Four streets. Three. Two. Pedalling away, racing your tired shadow. That's not the point. You're supposed to bring something back, that's the point. Something every day, just something small. A note. A stone. A chocolate. Put the bike on its stand under the apple tree on Weichselstrasse, reach up and stretch, a little higher, and there it hangs: just right, big and red with a fleck of green. It has to be flawless. Undamaged. Further on, the last houses. The last few letters. The end up ahead. Number thirty-four. The black wooden house with the moss in the cracks and the plastic pond. Four frogs with yellowing crowns, but no water, not for years. The last letter. The sunlight flashing through the hedge. There's still time. And it's downhill all the way home.

Heide Friedland

There were sixty-seven, if I remember rightly. One more or less doesn't make any difference. The man with the brooms doesn't count. He always carried two brooms around with him. He used to prop them up against the bar in the Golden Moon, and when he'd had a few too many, which was quite often, he'd start talking to them. He called them Charlie and Taff and sometimes he would run his fingers through their bristles. He doesn't count.

The last one was a retired policeman who was staying in Paulstadt to wind up his late sister's affairs. He used to sit in Lehmkuhl's café in the afternoon and order open-faced sandwiches. He had a white walrus moustache that caught the crumbs. Our love story lasted less than a week, then his sister's business was sorted. After he left, we wrote to each other a few times. The last letter I got was from his daughter: *I wanted to let you know that our beloved father . . . I'm sure he would have wanted . . . After all, you were . . .* etc. There were no more after that.

I'd had a fling with another walrus moustache twenty years earlier. He was staying at the Black Buck for a few days, then he had to go overseas. That's what he said, anyway. Every morning he would spend half an hour in front of the mirror stroking and tweaking his moustache, which was prodigious and waggled up and down when he spoke. It looked as if a living creature were squatting under his nose. But I would really have liked to see him again. He had nice legs.

Then there was the drawing teacher who suddenly turned weird in the middle of a class, drew a stripe across his forehead in oils and then jumped out of the window. The classroom was on the first floor and he broke both his legs, but there was clearly something wrong with his head, and he left Paulstadt as a screaming king in a white carriage.

And Lennard – he was a romantic. Scattered rose petals on the bed, said nice things about my eyes and forehead and so on. He had a bald head that he shaved every day, dabbing on scented cream and polishing it with a little sponge till it gleamed like a pink balloon.

The Field

With Hermann I used to go into the fields. He said he loved the rustling of the corn, but I think there was another reason. He always hummed the same tune on the way back into town. I never found out what it was. I often asked him, but he said he didn't know, either.

Roland I met in winter. He almost knocked me over on the street. Then he stood there looking down at the ground. Snowflakes clung to his eyebrows. I'm not sure he ever looked me in the eye. I can't remember what colour his were, anyway. In fact, I can't remember anything about him except his name and those big, trembling flakes above his eyes. I believe I wiped them away with my fingertips, and that was his undoing.

Most of them, though, I had in summer. I liked it when they sweated, and I liked to smell them. Sometimes, on those warm summer evenings, everything seemed so easy. You could open the windows wide and do it surrounded by the noises of the town.

I don't like cold feet. Henri's were very cold. He really made an effort, more than most of the others, but nothing he did could make up for the coldness of his feet. The touch of his toe was an Arctic blast that caught you unawares and instantly turned your body and the bed and the room and the birch tree and the birds and the clouds outside your window to brittle, splintering ice.

And Hans was too old for me. Too old to meet again, anyway. He reminded me of someone, I don't remember who, but I swear it wasn't my father. And I felt a bit sorry for him. He sat on the edge of the bed; his legs were very thin, his toenails cracked and yellow. And he had long white hair on his back. He asked me three times whether his white hair bothered me, and the third time I said yes.

The most beautiful of all was Frederik. He was so beautiful I could hardly believe it the first time I saw him. He had big, dark eyes, but when he looked at you it was as if he was just looking in a mirror. I never once saw him laugh. His heart was poisoned, and so was his liver, later on. I don't think it was the alcohol that killed him. He died of his own poison.

With Ralph it lasted almost two years. He wasn't a real man – that is, not what people usually think of as one. I liked that. His lack of manliness gave me a strange kind of security. Yet he was a lawyer. The most feared lawyer in town, in fact. At home he lay beside me and buried his thin, mouse-like face in my arms and was overwhelmed with shame. He said he was ashamed of everything he did and was, ashamed of his very existence. Shame had crept inside him long ago like a fog and had been slowly and steadily corroding his heart ever since. That's what he said. Out in the world, though, he was different. He took hundreds of people to court, regardless of whether or not they deserved it. In the courtroom they all danced to his tune and he stood there, grinning, and was as tall as the ceiling.

Sigmund would have liked to be a painter. He went through unbelievable quantities of paint, but never sold a single painting. He gave me a watercolour once but you couldn't make anything out. It was propped against the wardrobe in my entrance hall for ages, then at some point it was gone.

Klaus smelled bad. I think he had stomach problems. He sometimes read to me in the evening from one of his books. If he sat in the armchair by the fire and I stayed at the table, it was bearable.

I wanted to get engaged to Hilmar. Seriously. But he refused to buy rings, so I ended it. He went and picked up one of the dolled-up waitresses from the Pastry Cook café and married her three weeks later. The two of them pottered around town for years, side by side, like a pair of sad birds. I think he died before her.

Kurt was a dreamer. He had muscles like a bull and his fingernails were always dirty. But his eyes seemed to reflect the sky, presumably even when he was lying under one of his cars (which he usually was).

Paul wasn't bad, either. When he was drunk, he used to say he'd drained the marshes and in doing so had saved the town. I gave him a photo. It showed me as a child, in black and white, with plaits and a serious expression.

My first was seventeen, two years older than me. Everything about him smelled of ink. He wrote poems that didn't rhyme and made no sense, either. They were word sculptures, he said. He ended up working at the town hall. He was in charge of the heating system, and sometimes sat in the porter's lodge.

Lennie, Hagen, Wilfried, Werner I, Werner II, Helmut, Tom, Rudolph, Christian I, Christian II, Christian III, the gardener, the doctor, the short guy, the guy with the briefcase, the pudgy guy, the man that no one saw. It was astonishing: one would only just have left and the next would already be there. Yet I didn't have much to offer. I wasn't even that pretty. Basically, though, men don't care what a woman looks like. They want to feel good about themselves, that's all.

One of them saved me. I've forgotten his name. No matter what I do, his name simply will not come to mind. He saved me because he left.

Jonathan was religious. In the beginning he talked about God incessantly; then I told him my views on the matter and he stopped bothering me with it. Secretly, I envied him. He would go to church, and when he came back it was as if his face was still bathed in the light from the stained-glass windows. When the priest burned it all down, Jonathan lay in my bed and didn't move for three days. Then he got up, and our relationship was over.

Oswald had long, strong arms, but he didn't know how to use them. They hung at his sides as if they were sewn onto his shoulders. But arms are important. They don't necessarily have to be strong, but they must be able to hold you. You can lie in a man's arms and still feel completely alone. He holds you tight, and he feels great, because inside he's all toasty and warm. But none of this warmth reaches the outside, and everything about you contracts and curls up tighter and tighter, until you've shrunk to a cold, hard marble stuck in the crook of his arm. And then someone comes and puts his arm around you, and his touch is like a memory. It's as warm as a summer's day in the fields. Most men's arms mean nothing to you. Some you would like to live in.

There was one who smelled of burnt wood. And one who twisted his knee proposing to me. And one who was always whistling 'La Paloma'. And a fat one who could hardly get up the stairs and would still be panting long after he'd lain down on the carpet. And Edward. And Hannes. And four Martins. And Heiner. And Heiner's father. And Gerhard. And Burkhart. And Fritz. And the man with the three-legged dog. They hated each other. I think the man had cut off the dog's leg when it was still a puppy. Later, the dog mauled his forearm to shreds. Apparently they lie side by side in the same grave. There were quite a lot of weirdos in my life; I must have attracted them somehow. My mother used to say: there are a few misshapen turnips in every field, but they all taste the same.

You weren't a weirdo. You weren't even a little bit crazy. You weren't beautiful or interesting or remarkable in any other way. You were *normal*. I never understood how it was possible for you to happen to me. You said, come on, I'll buy you an ice cream. It wasn't even properly spring yet. Afterwards, we went to yours. It was nothing special, and you had ten pale blue shirts hanging in your wardrobe. I don't know why we met up again, or when exactly everything changed. When did you say it for the first time? When did I hear it for the first time? When did I start doing everything in my power to touch your heart? Perhaps it was just loneliness. Perhaps it was your arms. I can't say for certain. Do you know? If you know, don't tell anyone. Promise me you won't tell anyone!

Franz Straubein

A house. Four floors. Forty-eight stairs. One doormat: *Welcome home*. One table with knotholes. Two televisions (one black and white). One painting of sea, clouds and fishing boat. One other painting, of wildflowers. Twenty-two ring binders. One box with (approximately) three hundred photos. Nine windows, no curtains. Three antennas. One bird skeleton. One single look into the distance. Six degrees below zero and the heating gone again. One pale blue cup. Four tiny, delicate cracks. A lot of broken pieces. Two hundred and fifty square metres of garden. Eighty square metres of concrete. Three cars. Six insurance policies. No payout. Twelve times in hospital. Seventeen relatives. Three wives. One love. One son, who doesn't know me. Sixty-eight years and three months. One entry in the town records. One name. Two—

Karl Jonas

'There's going to be rain.' We all raise our heads and see the big black cloud approaching. Its shadow falls across Father's face, across the house, across the flat land beyond. I think the landscape goes on like this for ever, and it all belongs to us. I am five or six. We go on working in silence. Father leads the team pulling the potato spinner; the older men dig the potatoes out of the ground with forks and hoes. We younger ones and the women collect them in baskets. We're all sweating, especially the horses. The air is damp and warm and weighs heavily on the fields. And then it starts to rain. We run towards the house, and I'm laughing, holding my mother's hand, because the big, warm drops are splashing onto my forehead. When I look back, Father is still standing in the field. He is holding the reins in his fists. His face is upturned to the sky, rain pouring down his cheeks.

Later, at table, he's angry. He curses the rain. And he curses our land. He says it's no good. The earth swallows the water and spits it out again at will. It lacks solidity, it's just a sandy sponge riddled with marshes where nothing but flies' eggs grow. He bangs his fist on the table. Then he falls silent, and we all fall silent, and outside in the darkness the rain sweeps over the fields.

We were four families. We made the land. We solidified and drained it, we built the dykes and, later on, laid the pipes. The town is built on our land. Our name is older than all the houses. It's older than every cobblestone. Every spring, when the water rises up out of the ground and floods the cellars, it pushes a few old bones out of the earth. Mother used to say that there were more bones under the town than there were stones.

Some summers there's no sign of the water. It seems to have seeped away for ever; the wind drives the dust over the fields, and our faces and the animals' backs and the metal machinery are coated in dust. Every now and again the children look at each other and laugh. They draw stripes on their dusty faces with their fingers and laugh so hard they have to clutch their sides.

And then the water is back again. A few hours of rain is all it takes to squeeze out the sponge beneath our feet. The clouds blow over, but the mud stays. Then you're wading through dirt, boots heavy with earth, black flies buzzing at the back of your neck. And the earth sticks to the potatoes as well. They're twice as heavy as usual and worth less than half as much.

The land's no good, but it's all we've got.

My parents grew old, then they died, and one after another everyone left. When the last of my brothers went, he said to me, 'What are you staying here for? Come with me, before you get eaten by the flies!'

I thought: let them go if they want. More land for me. It'll pay off. Everything pays off eventually. I bought them out, said goodbye and wished them all the best. I was the farmer now. And I could be stubborn. I kept going back to the bank until I got what I wanted. I bought machinery. I employed seasonal workers. I filled in the old dykes and laid drainage pipes. Then I extended the house, built two garages, the big silo, and a corrugated-iron hangar for five hundred turkey chicks. I bought a dark-blue suit and went to a tea dance at the Black Buck, where I found a wife. She couldn't work, but we had five children together, three of whom survived. At some point they left home. If nothing's happened to them, they're still alive.

'Perhaps this will all still amount to something,' I said to my wife.

'Yes,' she said. 'Of course it will.'

But she didn't believe it. And she was right. The drainage pipes helped for a while, but then everything flooded again, and we were wading through an ankle-deep lake where the potatoes drowned. And then there were weeks when everything dried out and the earth split open, sharp-edged cracks appeared everywhere, and there was no water to save the fields, not a drop. There was the time of flies and the time of dust.

Sometimes a hole would appear in the middle of a field. In a single night it would fill up with water that had vanished by the following day.

The turkey chicks were a non-starter. They contracted a disease, and as we were shooing them from one half of the hangar to the other for their vaccinations, a partition fell down and we lost the overview. So we vaccinated all of them again. I think it was the vaccine they died of, not the disease. Those were not good times.

And then my wife left. That was just how it was. My wife left, and I acted as if I didn't care, and maybe I didn't. Now I was alone with my land and my hands and a huge, empty corrugated-iron hangar that sang at night in the wind.

I was all right with that. I sat on my front doorstep, watching the wind, and had the sense that everything was coming together in me. I was my father, I was my grandfather, I was his father and his father and his father. I was the last and the first in this long line of people, and in the ground beneath my feet the roots were loosening and I was all right with that.

I was tired.

I knew it was all over. No one has the strength to get a ninety-hectare clay and gravel sponge to prosper. All there was left for me to do was seal the windows and doors to stop the flies getting into the house.

They came one hot summer morning. The mayor and two men in suits. I don't know who those two were or what they were called. They were just men in grey suits, sweating like the horses in the sun. I'd seen the big black car jolting up the track from a long way off, and when it stopped the blue of the sky was reflected in the windscreen. We went inside and sat at the table. The mayor asked, 'How long have we known each other now?'

'As far as I'm aware, we don't know each other at all,' I said.

'It must be thirty years. At least. That's a long time, isn't it?'

I stared at the pattern on the tablecloth. It was lots of little overlapping rectangles. The others also seemed to be inspecting the tablecloth. I hadn't offered them anything to drink, not because I was rude, I just didn't have any clean glasses. The mayor cleared his throat and leaned towards me. His hair was stuck to his forehead, as if he'd been running in the rain.

'Let's talk man to man, Jonas,' he said. 'We haven't come all the way out here to see you just so we can enjoy the nice weather, because this isn't nice weather at all, am I right?'

'That depends,' I said. 'On how you look at it.'

'We didn't come to keep you company all morning, either. As mayor, one ought perhaps to do that sort of thing every now and then, but there just isn't time, you understand. Time slips away like nobody's business, and before you know it the day's over. How much time have you got left, Jonas?'

'Just say what it is you want, Mr Mayor.'

He leaned back again, wiped the sweat from his forehead and said, 'I'd like to buy your land.'

'I wouldn't do that if I were you,' I said. 'The land's no good.'

'It's good for us,' said the mayor. 'It's the right size, it's close enough to town, and the road goes right down the middle.'

'What road? There isn't a road.'

'There will be a road.'

I really didn't know the mayor. I'd heard of him; my wife had talked about him. She'd said he was just like his father: vain, corrupt, greedy, and a skirt-chaser. She was probably right, but I didn't care. The way he sat there, sweating, at my kitchen table, I kind of liked him. It occurred to me that perhaps there were a few clean glasses in one of the cupboards after all, and I asked if they would like something to drink.

'We don't want to put you to any trouble,' said the mayor. 'We want to buy your land, that's all.'

I stood up, got the glasses and a jug of water, and they drank it all. I said, 'Ten thousand.'

They sat there, in their suits, their turkey necks chafed red by their ties, and stared at me.

'For all of the land?' asked the mayor.

'Yes,' I said. 'It's no good. It's full of marshes.'

'Yes, that's true,' said the mayor.

'And then it's all dry and hard, like a brick worn away by the wind.'

'Terrible,' said the mayor.

'So,' I said. 'Ten thousand for the land.'

'Let's shake on it,' said the mayor.

'And five hundred thousand for the poultry hangar.'

'What?'

'Five hundred thousand for the hangar.'

'You think you're smart, huh?'

'No, I think I'm pretty stupid. The only thing I ever learned was how to dig potatoes out of the ground. Nothing else. But the thing is: for some reason, you want my land. I don't know what that reason might be, but it's obviously good enough for you to come out here in this heat in your ties and your patent leather shoes. The land's no good, but it belongs to me.'

'Is there any more water?' asked the mayor. I fetched another jug and they drank it all.

'The water tastes a bit peculiar,' said the mayor. I said nothing. He kept trying different approaches. He badgered me, got angry, tried being threatening, then friendly. But I said nothing. He gave up. We shook hands, and everything happened the way it did.

When I went into town, I didn't look back. I used the money to buy myself a life residency at the Sunset Retirement Home. It was worth it, because I lived another fifteen years and more. My room was small; it had yellow wallpaper with an almost invisible pattern. It was a stiff sort of paper, and it felt good when I stroked it with my fingers. I didn't like to go out; the town was too loud for me and the pavements too slippery. I stayed in my room, just sitting there. I liked it that the room was small. I'd spent my whole life staring into the distance. I barely thought about my previous life. I barely thought about the world outside. When I heard about the accident, I couldn't help laughing. I felt sorry for the three who were buried under the rubble, but I'd told them the truth about the land. It's no good.

The days were fine, but I struggled with the nights. I couldn't sleep in the dark. Once, I felt afraid. A noise had woken me, and I sensed that I was no longer alone in the room. I was sure I could hear someone breathing in the dark. I crept out of bed and sat on the chair by the window, but I didn't open the curtains. It was quiet again. I rested my head and arms on the window ledge. I sat like that for a while, listening, and then something inside me began to crumble. I slid off the chair and broke apart like a clod of dry earth.

Susan Tessler

'You dice the potatoes, chop the onions and brown them in butter in a hot frying pan with a pinch or two of coarse-grained flour,' said Henriette. 'But use waxy potatoes. And they have to be diced,' she added, firmly.

'Hold on,' I said. 'Why's it so important to dice them?'

'It looks better,' she said.

'That's all?'

'That's all.'

Henriette was a little, grumpy old woman who always knew best, and whose propensity for angry outbursts and sudden foul temper was prevented from achieving its full expression only by her frailty. She herself saw this differently. She described herself as a part-time enthusiast. And it was true that, depending on her frame of mind, she was also capable of seeing something good and beautiful in everything. She even speculated that there was hidden beauty in the faded wallpaper, presumably once lime-green, on the wall in our ward doctor's waiting room, where we spent so many hours sitting next to each other. 'Do you see the vine tendrils up there?' she asked me, the first time we met. 'They are tendrils, aren't they? Or do you just say vines?'

'They're neither tendrils nor vines,' I replied. 'They're just cracks in the ceiling. They really ought to renovate in here.'

'Ah, now I remember! You see the recurring up and down, that undulating movement?' she cried, enthusiastically. 'Of course they're tendrils. No doubt about it. What's your name?'

'Tessler,' I said. 'Susan Tessler.'

'My name is Henriette. Just Henriette. I've let go of the surname. You let go of everything in time. Shall we shake hands?'

We arrived at the sanatorium at around the same time. I think I was there first. It was spring, and lilac and laburnum were in blossom in the little park outside my window. My room was light and airy (it presumably still is), with a view of the garden, and a French balcony that I only ever used at night, to cool the chocolate I'd smuggled past the nurses. The sanatorium allowed its residents to bring their own furniture and personal items. I didn't need anything from home. I was perfectly happy with the standard furnishings:

wardrobe, bookshelf, night stand, table, two chairs, a bed. The bed was a metal apparatus, a piece of equipment with pedals that allowed it to be raised or lowered at will and tilted in all directions. The bars at the foot end creaked with every movement, but the mattress was soft. I had a floor lamp, a bedside rug, and two white porcelain vases. I made sure there were always two apples or a few nuts on the table. I never ate them, but I liked to look at them, and sometimes I would toss them out of the window and watch them roll across the lawn and come to rest in the shadow of the trees, where they lay until they were removed by one of the gardeners.

There was nothing that I missed. To be honest, I was glad I'd left my old things in the Paulstadt apartment, where they presumably sat in dusty silence for quite some time. Objects had long since lost their meaning. Henriette called them 'the clutter of our lives'.

I'd already seen her many times before our first conversation in the waiting room. She was unusually small and thin, always elegantly dressed, and wore her long white hair in a bun at the back of her head that she called a snowball. Everything about her was somehow crooked and contorted: her back, her legs, her nose, her hands. Her face was cross-hatched with fine wrinkles, and on her décolletage, right over her delicate breastbone, she had a scar at least fifteen centimetres long in the shape of a horseshoe.

She always sat in the same corner of the common room. She drank dark red tea and always had a book open in her lap, although everyone knew that her eyes had clouded over long ago and she could hardly even tell faces apart. I remember the slight maliciousness that overcame me during one of our first encounters. I had, of course, heard about Henriette's poor eyesight (there are no secrets in the sanatorium concerning residents' state of health and vulnerabilities), and yet – or perhaps for that reason – I asked her what the book in her lap was about. To my amazement, she told me the story from beginning to end. It was about an explorer who was consumed with ambition, and about his adventures in the hot desert sands. She spoke emphatically, elaborated every detail, and recounted the entire story all the way to its dramatic end, by which time the tea was cold. I could have slapped her.

'Tumour as well?' she asked me once.

'Liver,' I replied. 'And now the kidneys, too.'

'Mine's in my head,' she said. 'Everything that's bad for you starts in the head. Where are you from?'

'Paulstadt,' I said.

'Sorry?'

'Paulstadt,' I repeated.

'Good grief,' she said, raising one of her finely plucked eyebrows. 'Really?'

Her arrogance annoyed me, because I liked Paulstadt. It was my childhood home, the home of my youth, and I said so. She closed her book with a soft brush of her hand and looked at me with her little, half-blind eyes. 'I know I can be a fool sometimes,' she said. 'Stupid and supercilious. But I'll be damned if I'll apologize. You understand that, don't you, my dear?'

Little, thin Henriette, almost transparent by the end. Her shins like narrow wooden slats beneath her dress. The gnarled hands on the back of her book. The dark, mottled face, almost smaller than the snowball behind it. The fluttering, permanently reddened eyelids. Her gaze, which seemed to retreat further into her eyes with every day that passed.

'Paulstadt, Paulstadt,' she said, another time, seemingly lost in thought. 'Isn't that the place where that dreadful thing happened?'

'Yes,' I answered. 'Terrible.'

'They wanted to put in a tram line, but people opposed it, didn't they?'

'Sorry?'

'Those idiots just opposed it!'

'Yes. Possibly. I don't remember now.'

We fell silent for a while. Suddenly she gave a jolt and straightened up in her chair.

'Just imagine,' she said. 'A tram! With tracks and dinging bells and all the trimmings!'

'Yes,' I said. 'Really terrible!'

People put their heads together in the common room and corridors. The rumour was going around that Henriette was a Jew. One of the nurses had heard her talking in her sleep. It had been more like babbling, though, she said, completely incomprehensible, and mixed with the grinding of Henriette's remaining teeth, but she was sure she'd heard a few words of Hebrew. I didn't join in the gossip. I could have asked Henriette, of course, but I never had the nerve. And what difference would it have made?

I know now that she made up the story of the ambitious desert explorer as she was telling it. She had that gift. You never knew with her what was true and what was not. But she told such good stories that you just wanted to listen, either way. There was a kind of rivalry among the female residents as to who got to sit next to her in the afternoon. I was usually quickest. The trick was already to be seated in the common room before she came in. Then we would sit together, she would tell her stories and I would listen. Sometimes we would both fall asleep. Her snores found their way into my dreams, as the puttering of boat engines in foreign harbours, as the rise and fall of a forest floor cracking open, as my father's snoring, quiet and throaty, somewhere in the darkness of an apartment abandoned long ago.

'I will never address the unfathomable out there with the word God. If I ever do, it's the medicine talking, do you understand?'

We didn't talk much about our past. The essentials were soon ticked off: where we'd lived, employment, husbands (dead), children (none), patterns of life and convictions (varying). Stuff like that. I think we felt our past had been exhausted in the telling. It consisted of nothing now beyond faded pictures, names and dates that could no longer be brought to life.

We preferred to concern ourselves with the present. We talked about the other residents, about the nurses, the doctors, the kitchen staff, or the pigeons on the gutters and the gravel paths in the garden. Sometimes we told each other dreams. But what we liked best was to talk about food. Henriette loved hearty meals, whereas I preferred the fine pastry dishes I'd learned from old cookery books. She wanted to hear about these pastry books. I had to describe the photos to her in detail, and recite the recipes in their entirety, if possible, which of course it wasn't. So I too began to make things up. I said, 'You need two hundred and eighty grams of butter, one hundred and forty grams of icing sugar, two or three egg yolks, a small handful of ground almonds, a bit of lemon peel, two hundred grams of flour, and jam, of course (preferably blackcurrant). You have to stir the butter vigorously with the icing sugar and the yolks, *but vigorously means vigorously, otherwise it won't work, you see*, so you stir vigorously for at least twenty minutes, then you sprinkle in the ground almonds and the grated lemon peel and keep stirring; now you add the flour, stir it in *vigorously* again for a few minutes, then you put a quarter of the batter into the tin (you don't need to grease the baking paper, the butter in the pastry is enough), spread the jam on top, then you distribute the rest of the batter with a nozzle in a lattice over the cake, though of course you can always do some other pattern, it'll still taste the same, then you decorate the side with the rest of the batter and put it all in the oven, bake at one hundred and eighty degrees for forty to forty-five minutes, finally release the cake gently from the tin and sprinkle it with icing sugar.'

'Even more sugar?' she asked, her eyes closed.

'Yes,' I said. 'But it has to be icing sugar. And use a sieve. You definitely need a kitchen sieve.'

'Ah,' she said. 'A fine kitchen sieve?'

'The finest sieve you can lay your hands on!'

And so the summer passed. We spent some lovely times together. Yet the main thing I remember is a feeling of sadness. In fact, I remember my whole life as if through a veil of sadness. Sadness is all that's left. But perhaps it could be worse. For a long time I tried to tell myself that we don't die, we just leave this world. Death is just a word. But that's not true.

In early October she grew too weak to make her way to the communal area, and I spent the afternoons in her room. It was even emptier than mine. There wasn't even a table, and only one chair. In a corner stood a suitcase. Henriette said it contained letters and a few books, the only acceptable luggage for any journey. She lay in bed with her torso half-raised on a support pillow, a small, malicious queen. It looked as if she might at any time get lost in her own bed. But she laughed again and bit into her baguette sandwich, which she dunked in the cup of milk on her bedside table with trembling fingers. We had the newspapers brought to us, and I read to her. She often ranted about what was going on in the world, and when she did she would scold so loudly and with such fury that one of the nurses would burst in to tell us to be quiet.

'What can I do, damn it – I'm temperamental!' Henriette would cry, trembling with agitation.

She liked to pick fights with the nurses. If she was in pain, or just in a bad mood, she would shout the most obscene insults at them the moment they entered the room. Secretly, though, she liked these young women who moved among us ghosts like determined angels. On good days she would even compliment them, admire their figures, their smooth skin or the clear whites of their eyes. And the nurses liked her, too, not only because of the tips she handed out on any pretext. All of us had money, more or less (I'd made mine cutting and stencilling metal sheets, Henriette hers, as she put it, with 'three marriages and a great deal of patience'), but with her it was different. There was something about her . . . I have no memory of my mother, who died when I was just a girl, but I imagine that she was like Henriette.

'Sssh, be quiet a moment! Don't you see the clouds out there? From here it looks as if they're just passing slowly and quietly overhead. Yet in fact they're racing across the sky, and there's roaring and thundering and crashing all about them. The trees have noticed them already. They're bowing down before them.'

Autumn progressed, and Henriette lost her strength. The support pillow was removed, and she was only able to leave the bed in the arms of a male nurse. Mostly she lay on her side with her eyes closed, or gazing out of the window to where the November wind was sweeping the last leaves from the trees. She could barely see, but on quiet nights she fancied she could hear the leaves falling. We still enjoyed talking and laughing. I no longer remember when we did that for the last time.

Her clothes were put away in the storeroom beside the bathroom; she always wore a silk nightdress now that shimmered in the moonlight as if made of polished ice.

They hooked her up to a quietly beeping apparatus, and her dose of medication was increased. She slept almost all the time; sometimes she groaned and her breath rattled in her sleep. Her voice sounded distorted and strange, like the voice of a hoarse child.

I can't say where I found the strength to keep watch for so long beside her bed. I think it felt as if time stood still while I was sitting with her. There was no clock in the room, and I hadn't owned one for some time. It only occurs to me now that I didn't see a single clock during my whole time in the sanatorium. Time seemed to have become irrelevant – and, on the other hand, too precious to measure in mere minutes, hours, days.

Sometimes I held her hand, that withered, wrinkled hand. Sometimes I stroked her hair with my fingers. The nurses had loosened her bun and her hair lay long and dishevelled on the pillow.

Once she woke and raised her head. 'Who are you?' she asked me in a clear voice. I stared at her. The question seemed monstrous.

'I don't know,' I said.

She lowered her head again and went back to sleep. Perhaps she hadn't even been properly awake. I went to my room, went to bed, and cried half the night.

Henriette died ninety-three days after my arrival and twenty-six days before me. She was my friend for sixty-seven days. She was the best friend I had in my life.

On one of her last nights, I was sitting beside her as she slept. The previous evening, the doctors had decided to increase her dose. We must all endure a certain amount in our lives, the consultant had said, but it doesn't have to be more than necessary. Her breathing was scarcely audible, but it was calm, and I was looking out of the window to where the bare trees reached up into the night sky. Her handbag was open on the window ledge, and her belongings were laid out beside it at regular intervals, as if someone had tried to put them in order. A lipstick, a gold powder compact, writing paper, a coin purse, a nail file and a thin, rather worn leather writing case. Henriette's breath rattled quietly, and I felt a sudden rush of anger. I was angry with the little wizened, shrunken woman at whose bedside I had spent so many hours, and who was now withdrawing from me and leaving me nothing but a rattling breath.

The anger ebbed as quickly as it came. Her breath was

calm again now, and even. The only possible way not to become ridiculous in old age is to acknowledge one's own ridiculousness, she once said. I got up and went to the window. I spotted the initials on her leather writing case: H.L. I opened the case. It contained a few documents, medical records, certificates and loose papers. Right at the bottom was her passport. The pages were covered with brightly coloured stamps. Henriette seemed to have spent her whole life travelling. The photo showed her as a young woman. She'd not been beautiful then, either, but her hair was black and shoulder-length and she was looking into the camera with her chin held high. Her décolletage with the scar was concealed by a big black shawl. At the bottom of the page were her personal details: full name, place of birth, nationality, distinguishing marks, the usual. My gaze snagged on her date of birth. I faltered, and tears sprang to my eyes. I felt faint, and clung to the window sill in order to stay upright. Henriette was four years younger than me.

I looked across at her. She lay in the bed, her body bathed in moonlight as if covered with snow. I couldn't see the movement of her breath; everything about her appeared frozen except her eyes, which darted about under the lids and seemed blindly to follow my every move as I put her things back in the bag and opened the window wide to let in the night air.

Peter Lichtlein

BAM! and off I run. Once I'm running you can't stop me. No one can. I'm big and strong and I know things. I know exactly where I want to go. Down the corridors, down the steps, across the playground, through the gate, here I'm still running but in the streets I'm the wind. The dust doesn't bother me. The dogs don't bother me. Nor do the cars or the pigeons or the houses that stand in front of the sky and look as if they're still growing taller. I know there are people here, but I don't see them, and the people don't see me, and soon they won't be there any more. But it's only when the houses behind me look like tiny pebbles that I slow down. And then I drop onto the grass and lie on my back, and the Earth's heart is beating under me.

When I'm calm again, I stand up. Now I can walk and I don't have to keep looking back. Not far now. Past the fences, across the old sewage pipe I used to be able to crawl through, and on through the bushes and sharp reeds, and then I can already see the trees and the pool, and it's funny: although I know everything out here is continually growing and breaking and blossoming and dying, everything looks exactly the same as last time.

The pool is my friend. Only no one knows. I don't want anyone to know. It's a secret. I'm a secret. It's better if no one knows me. The earth all around is soft and dark and wet. But I've got a trick: I pull out a few handfuls of reeds and spread them on the earth. That's my bed.

My mother's forbidden me to go to the pool. But I won't let her forbid me. I come here a lot. No one disturbs me here, and I can just sit and look and think, or not look and not think, whichever I want. My mother doesn't understand that.

My mother is beautiful. She has a big face and big hands. She cut up a rabbit in the bathtub once. Its blood was black and, although I couldn't help thinking about its eyes, its meat tasted good. My mother likes talking about food. And then I talk about it, too, because I know she likes it. We sit at the table and talk about the bread. We say that you can scratch the burnt bits off the crust with a knife and it's nice and soft inside. We talk about the meat, as well. We say that the meat used to belong to an animal, and will never completely belong to us. If for once we're not talking about food, my mother says other things, too.

My mother says:

What have you done to your hands?

Go to sleep now.

Three angels are sitting on the window ledge. The first has sleep in his pocket. The second, happiness. And the third watches over the other two.

Stand there.

Stop it.

Don't be cross with me.

The God of love is not that loving, and the devil blows out the stars.

School. Potato. Man.

Things like that.

The water is black as rabbit's blood. And that's the nicest thing about it. It's black and quiet and deep. I know how deep it is. It's so deep it can swallow the sun. There are toads, too. My mother says toads are lucky, but I don't think she really knows. I suppose you can eat toads if you're hungry, but I've never dared to eat one. I've just caught one from time to time and thrown it in the water. They have yellow eyes. People think the water reflects the stars at night. But I know the yellow lights in the pool are just toads' eyes.

I'm a toad. I have yellow eyes, a sticky tongue and a dark, warty back. I just have to protect my belly, it's pale and soft and you can prod it with a stick until it bursts and the life pours out of it. The flies like the life.

Winter is no time for toads. It's cold, and the trees are

like the bars of the school gate, thin and bare and black. It's better in summer. Then I inhale the sunlight and there's humming and buzzing everywhere, and the flies and bees and worms are my food and I don't have to dig a burrow to sit in, cold and stiff and waiting for the thaw.

I don't like the school gate. I don't like the playground. I don't like the benches. The bell. The voices, high and low. The shouting. The whispers. I don't like any of it, but I like the teachers least of all. They have grey faces and grey hands that they use to point at things that have nothing to do with me. The teachers can say what they like to me; if I don't want to do something, I don't do it. Or I don't even hear it. I block my ears with thoughts that don't upset me.

One of them slapped me once, with the flat of his hand: thwack! He shouldn't have done that. Why didn't he pull his hand back again afterwards? Maybe he wanted to stroke the pain away, but it didn't even hurt. Anyway, he kept his hand on my cheek and gave me this look. So I bit him. And didn't let go. I wanted to, but I couldn't. My teeth clamped down, and his blood tasted sweet, but kind of salty, too. I know he screamed, but I didn't hear it. I think someone forced my jaw open, with a tool or something, I don't know, and then they pulled me away. It was only much later, when it was all over and I was lying beside the pool, alone again, that I was sorry. But why did he hit me? He shouldn't have done. Or should at least have pulled his hand away quicker.

The others are the others and I am me. The others have a lot to say, but they don't understand very much. I don't think I understand more than them, but I don't talk as much. I prefer to talk when I'm alone.

It's better at home. I can sit in my corner, imagining things. I imagine things, but I can't remember them. It's funny: the things are in my head and I'm in them at the same time. They're very clearly there. But as soon as my mother calls me, they're gone. I know they must have been nice, because I feel good afterwards.

My mother goes to work. She goes into a big hall and stacks metal sheets on shelves that are so high they go all the way up to the roof. She has a long ladder. I've always wanted to climb up a long ladder like that, but my mother won't let me. There are lots of things she won't let me do, because she's always frightened for me. She locked me in the broom cupboard once, just because she was frightened. I didn't mind. I feel at home in the dark. The darkness is warm, and bright around the edges. I lay down on the floor and imagined things until the door opened again. My mother stood in the doorway, crying. She looked even more beautiful than usual. She looked like an angel in the church window. But she was crying, and that was bad. What is it, Mama, I asked, what is it? But she didn't say anything, just went on crying. She took me in her arms and sat down with me on the kitchen floor. We sat like that for a long time;

the tiles were cool, and I could see a wisp of spider's web trembling under the cupboard.

It was all all right in the end.

I'd like to see a toad in winter. Toads in winter are alive and not alive. I imagine everything about them stiffening: their legs, their bellies, their heads. Their eyes are cold yellow stones. I imagine the blood freezes in their toad veins, and every movement cracks and crunches. In summer it's different; the toads pulsate and their bodies are firm and soft at the same time. I always pick them up by the leg, and they dangle, twisting and wriggling. I won't hurt you, I say, you can carry on. The toads don't say anything. I look at them, and then I throw them into the pool in a great big arc and there's a splash and they're gone.

I'm running into the wind. The fields are yellow and butterflies are dancing by the wayside. I'm running and my lungs are burning and I'm thinking about my mother. She doesn't know yet, because I don't know yet either. She's my mother. I am a toad. The wind is good. I can't feel my face. I run and run. The trees clutch at the sky and I can already smell the pool. The water is black and quiet. I lie down on my bed of reeds and wait. I wait until the sun disappears and the humming and chirping all around me stops. Night falls, but I'm not afraid. I imagine things and can't remember them. And then I get up and take off my clothes. I lay them out neatly in a row. I wouldn't want my mother to get cross.

The Field

The moon is hanging in a tree. I walk into the water and see my white feet shimmering below the surface. I keep walking. The water is very soft and the mud feels strange between my toes. I stop and listen. Then I just let myself fall forward. I don't feel the cold. I know that if I go deep enough I'll find the sun at the bottom.

Annelie Lorbeer

Being the oldest is not an achievement or an advantage. You die at a hundred and five the same as at eighty-five or thirty-two, and the price of a life that long is loneliness. Death is the same for everyone. It's just that the people standing beside the grave don't know that yet. I've often stood beside a grave, and it was never nice. The closest it might come would be in spring, if you don't know the deceased that well and the trees are blossoming and the birds chirping. Sometimes I imagined the birds in the trees were the souls of the dead. A nice idea, but nonsense, obviously.

On my hundredth birthday the mayor presented me with a certificate and a bunch of flowers. I don't know what it said on the certificate. During the ceremony in the garden, I was the only one allowed to sit. Sitting elevated me, as it were. I can't recall the music. In the old days there was always a band. Certificates without a band were pretty much unheard-of. But at some point music lost its importance.

Where I'm from, people didn't talk, they sang. It was nice. Although actually it got on my nerves, too, this singsong way of speaking. As if they were trying to sing reality away.

It was still nice, though.

No one came to my hundred-and-fifth. Even I wasn't fully there. I was just dreaming everything by then. Dreaming helped relieve the pain, and the weightiness of the soul.

Birthdays had long since ceased to matter to me by then. But I did want to experience death. I always was so curious.

Now I know what it's like. But I shan't say anything. It's forbidden to say anything about death. Death holds the truth, but you're not allowed to tell it. Lying is permitted, of course, but I don't want to lie. Anyway: no one came for me. I just fell out of life. We fall into life, and we fall out of it the same way. There's an opening, and you have to find it. Or you fumble around in the dark until you fall into it. One way or another, it always works.

First I was a child. Then a lady. Then a child again. I don't remember the bit in between. In any case, I was a beautiful lady. I had a certain elegance. Men would find themselves staring at my behind, and they would run after me. As did some women. I always had more of an eye for the women. They were more interesting, though the men smelled better. Like animals, but I couldn't now tell you which.

We had a canary. I don't remember what it was called. I think it was named after a minister. One morning the cage door was open and it was gone. Perhaps it tried to get to the trees. A few days later it was lying behind the curtain, small, stiff, still green. I said to Mama: look, it has claws like an animal! It seems until that moment I hadn't known that an animal was what it was.

The child and the woman were at war. I kept a piece of shrapnel in the chest of drawers in my room. They took it out of Papa's leg before they cut it off. I begged him to give me the splinter, and I kept it in a little box. Now you've locked up what's left of the war in that box, said Papa.

I can't recall his face. Where Papa's face once was, there's now just a blank. Or a shadow. Or a brightness. There are no faces any more.

He had a beard, I know that. Or maybe that was just the thorn hedge I would sometimes crawl into when I'd been naughty. They would always pull me out, bloody and naked, like a little Jesus. I wonder whether Jesus wept as much as I did. You couldn't have begrudged him that. Tears are the only benefit of pain.

I hardly remember anything about Mama, although she was with me longer. Just that she was warm, I remember that. Like fresh dough. And she collected kitchen knives.

They all sat in the chest of drawers, too, right next to the shrapnel box, the tea towels and a little wax saint. I think it was St George. He kills dragons in the name of Christ, so the kitchen knives should come in handy.

I didn't have children, and I never regretted it. Of course I would have been curious to know what it feels like when something of you extends into the future. But it didn't happen. Even though men were good to me. Which always surprised me, because I wasn't good to men. I didn't know them. I didn't really know anyone, not even myself. First I was too young. Then I was too proud. And, finally, too old. When you're old, you do start to understand a few things here and there, but they're no use to you any more.

Men weren't necessary to me. Sometimes I fell in love, but that happened with the gold weathercock on the town hall roof as well. Or the butterflies out on the paths through the fields. The butterflies were more necessary to me than all the men put together. They were also the best remedy for sadness. Very few men are a challenge; most are an imposition. They no longer know how to be great and melancholy.

I did know one melancholy man, just one. He was tall and had sharp knees, as befits a man. He had glasses, too, with lenses as thick as ice cubes. One time I put them on and lay down in front of him, half-blind. His heart almost burst with love. That's what he told me later. It's possible he would have been the one. But he went and died on me in his sleep.

After a certain age we think there's nothing left for us, but that's a mistake. As long as you're alive, there's always something to be done.

In general, though, ageing is a wretched business. The only good bit is that you get lighter. Thoughts are heaviest of all, and they're increasingly absent. Much falls away of its own accord. Everything, really.

My childhood memories have almost all gone. But there are still a few memories of the memories. And they're nice. Or at least they don't provoke any bad feelings.

My mother, where have you driven me?
My father, where are you taking me?

Is that a song?

Of course I would have liked to earn my own money. Instead, I was a lady. And this is not something that's actually desirable. When you're a lady, you're required to wear a permanent mask of make-up and pride that's so heavy it forces you into submission. The make-up and the pride pressed down on my shoulder blades and pushed them out of my back until they stuck out like clipped wings.

I would have liked to have streaked across the fields like the swallows. Or at least spun like the butterflies. They're all quite mad in spring. It's so beautiful you could almost believe in God. But that doesn't get you anywhere. The beauty of the butterflies needs no god. It actually exists.

I wasn't naturally elegant. As a girl, I would put on my mother's dancing shoes and walk up and down in front of the mirror. I was the tall, chubby type, a lump, really, and the shoes were two sizes too small. Up and down, up and down. There was nothing innate about it, like with Greta Garbo or Thea Bobrikova. My elegance was hard-won, but it sufficed for Paulstadt.

There were times when I would have liked to have prayed. *Be with me, O God*, or something along those lines. But I always stopped myself. I never talked to him, not even when I was in direst need. I didn't expect much of him.

As a girl you were practically dragged to church, unquestioning, uncomprehending. It was dreadful. I was affronted that I had to kneel. Mainly because it was humiliating, but also because of the marks it left on my tights. I used to make up stories in confession. They were so good and so depraved that I should have written them down and sold them instead of whispering them into the priest's cold ear. I wasn't a true sinner, of course. My sins were really pleasures. And God didn't care, anyway, because he doesn't exist. If he existed, he wouldn't need representatives on Earth. All that exists is human. God is not human, so he doesn't exist. Ever since persuading myself of that, I've made my peace with him. Throughout my life, I never feared God. My fears were of a different nature.

It's strange: I outlived everyone I knew. Those I didn't outlive, I didn't know. Now I can't even tell any more whether that's sad. I think I've lost my sense of humour.

Things disappear over time. It's called forgetting. I've forgotten a lot in a hundred and five years. But I know now that nothing is really lost. It's like with old pictures. Some you just put in a corner, some you cover up, some are painted over. I've painted over innumerable horrors. The fire and the attacks. The mockery and the loneliness. The tear-soaked pillows. The many, many contorted faces. Lastly, the slow, progressive transformation of my own face for the worse. I painted over all of them, but it didn't help.

When I was very young, a man said to me: Anni, you're so beautiful that I keep wanting to tell everyone about your beauty, but I don't have the words, so I'm keeping your beauty to myself. This, of course, was an outrageous cheek, and I told him I didn't want him and he should go away at once. Whereupon he walked out of town and shot himself in the head. He managed to make a mess of that as well. Instead of the thread of life, he severed his optic nerve, and was blind in both eyes from then on. But the nurse fell for him and went on to give him four children, at least one of whom would always lead him around town by the arm. He would hold his face up to the sky and smile. We no longer greeted each other, but I believe he was the happiest person I ever knew.

Basically, I understand nothing about love, and all I know about life is that it has to be lived. But at least I do now know a little about death. It puts an end to longing, and if you hold still it doesn't hurt at all.

Love. War. God. Father. Mother. Child. The hedge and the stealthiness. The flowers and white fear. Sharpness. Brightness. Snow. Summer lightning and the stockpot. Three more laughs, then it's over. The sun. The boat. The bird. Death.

There's so much that becomes undignified as the end approaches. Most things, actually. The injections and the household aids. The pills and the support corsets. The struggle for the last drop of vitality. And then those gowns that flutter open at the back with every step. A wrinkly bottom is as undignified as an improvised lie. Humans are nothing without dignity. We should maintain it ourselves for as long as possible. However, as the end approaches, dignity can only be bestowed upon us. It resides in others' eyes.

And now I've remembered a sentence. If I'm not mistaken, I was the one who thought it. It's a sentence that may not be for all eternity, but it is for the moment. You can't really ask for more than that.

First I was self, now I am world.

Hannes Dixon

The day it pleased Father Hoberg to set fire to the house of his Lord, I wrote the following headline: *Church burns, God lives!* It wasn't the best I've ever written, but it was good. Back then I still believed in truth, and that you can influence things for the better if you're sufficiently outraged. That fell by the wayside a bit later on. The world changed, truth always lagged behind reality, and outrage gave way to a not unpleasant sense of resignation.

Two and a half metres above me, carved in the cheapest limestone the town hall could get its hands on, it says: *Here lies Hannes Dixon, citizen and chronicler of Paulstadt.* This, of course, is utter nonsense. A chronicler is a pen-pusher who records events in chronological order, and a citizen pays taxes. I did neither.

I was a reporter. To be precise: I was the reporter, editor, typesetter, printer and publisher of Paulstadt's only newspaper, the *Paulstädter Bote*.

*

After more than five years of war, when instead of my father – whose face and voice I could no longer recall even then – all that came back was a typed, official letter that spoke of the performance of soldierly duties in keeping with the oath of allegiance for the greatness and future of our fatherland, as well as sincere condolences and irreplaceable loss, I hid behind the stairs to the coal cellar and drafted my first ever letter. It was addressed to my dead father, and I never had any intention of sending it. Where to? I put the letter in an envelope and buried it under the blackcurrant bush in our garden. Then I walked out into the fields, lay down in a furrow and wept until I felt as dry and brittle as the earth beneath me. It was a hot summer, and I was fourteen years old.

The mound of earth under the blackcurrants must have caught my mother's eye. She found the letter, and after reading it several times from beginning to end, as she told me later, she called me into the kitchen. She sat on her stool and scrutinized me. Something in her gaze had changed. I thought it seemed infinitely sad, but there was also something in it that made me take heart. I felt oddly tall and strong, yet at the same time I was ashamed of this feeling. She folded her arms across her chest. For a few moments all was quiet in the kitchen, then suddenly she said, 'You were the most wonderful child I could ever have imagined.'

I stared at her in alarm. She rested her hands in her lap.

'You're not a child any more,' she said. 'You may not be a man yet, but you're not a child any more. You're my son, and you've grown to be cleverer than I ever thought possible. You can think. You can see behind the curtain. You have potential – use it. Promise me you'll use your potential!'

Later I found out that, after the war, she made two copies of the letter and sent one to the readers' letters section of a national newspaper, and one to Paulstadt town hall 'for the personal attention of our esteemed mayor'. There was no response from the mayor, but the newspaper printed the letter, and my mother framed the page and hung it on the living-room wall, where it remained until her death, as a mark of her pride and a perpetual reminder to me. The reminder was: never be a worse person than you were at fourteen.

I realized back then what a great impression a few well-formulated sentences can make. I decided to dedicate my life to writing. To be precise, I decided to devote my life to writing down the truth, even though I didn't have the faintest idea what the truth might actually be. My father's death had seemed false to me somehow, a great big lie. What did the fact that someone had ended up in a muddy trench with their head shot to pieces have to do with heroism? And if someone was irreplaceable, as the lieutenant's letter had said, why did they put him in such a trench? And why was the talk all of the fatherland, when for ages now fathers had been returning from this mess confused or crippled, or not at all? These questions bothered me. And they prompted others. Questions I never had the nerve to ask my mother. Questions for my teachers, my schoolmates, the town hall, for every random passer-by who was able simply to walk across the street while my father was long since dead in the ground somewhere. And then there were questions for myself. Who was I? Who did I want to be? Who was I capable of being?

A fourteen-year-old boy in short trousers decides to look behind the curtain. He wants to be a journalist or writer – as yet, he sees no difference – one of the really great ones, anyway, or at least like the editors of the broadsheet newspapers they put out in Lehmkuhl's café, with articles attributed to initials like A.P. or K.T. or O.S. His chances are slim. Non-existent, in fact. But he has all these questions in his head, and the stubbornness of an old mule.

I got involved with the publication of our school magazine. We produced one hundred and thirty copies of the first edition; five students toiled away with carbon paper, making several copies at once. I was responsible for the 'Miscellaneous' section, which I filled with reports about playground fights and the weekly canteen menu. I always had a little pencil stuck behind my ear, which gave me an exhilarating air of industriousness. When I walked across the school playground, the others would watch me with a mixture of curiosity and contempt. 'Hey, Dixon, you sniffing around again?' they would shout. It was undignified and exciting.

After I finished school, I went to the local library and presented myself to the librarian. I said that I wanted to start a newspaper, and asked whether there might be someone who could help me. Oddly enough, she didn't laugh. She looked at me for a while, then said, 'Come with me.'

She opened a little door behind the stacks of cookery books, and a few steps took us down into the vaulted cellar. A single lightbulb hung from the ceiling, and our shadows roamed across walls that looked as if they had been carved straight out of the rock. The floor was carpeted in a thick layer of dust. 'There,' said the librarian, pointing to a corner. Between the boiler and piles of tattered books stood a huge black machine. 'Do you think you can do something with that?'

'Yes,' I said. 'I think I can.'

The machine was a Koenig & Bauer roller press that had once been used to print the parish newsletters. It was over a hundred years old, encrusted with a combination of lubricating oil and dust, and it took me almost a year to get it working. When it finally started up, with a rather vulgar noise, and the first pages rattled out from beneath the roller, I cheered so loudly that my voice cracked and a fine rain of plaster trickled from the ceiling.

Two months later, one icy winter's night just before my nineteenth birthday, I typeset the masthead of my new paper for the first time: *Der Paulstädter Bote*. Font: Walbaum Fraktur, bold, twenty-four point, anno 1812. My cloudy breath in the light from the bulb seemed to me like the spirit of a new age.

I ran the newspaper for thirty-nine years and took on a whole string of employees, people with enough enthusiasm, at least for a while, to believe in the power of the written word: pensioners, housewives, school dropouts, unskilled workers, mechanical engineers, unemployed teachers, slackers, blockheads, geniuses. They came and went. I stayed.

Thirty-nine years.

It's not true that time contracts when you look back on it. It was a long time, and it felt long to me. I did what I could. Nothing I printed went around the world; it all stayed in Paulstadt. But it makes no difference. Every moment contains the whole of time, and all the world is reflected in the shop windows of Marktstrasse. Once, right at the beginning, I ordered a copy of the *New York Times*. I wanted to get an idea of what others were doing. The newspaper came by post, with a week's delay. But it's not about discovering things in real time. If you want to know what's happening in real time, look in the mirror. The news only ever recounts what has already happened.

The Americans were good, but they weren't better than me. People's actions will always remain the same. The only difference is in the effects. And that too becomes relative with time.

Do you want to hear a story? Write it down. It's about the tram. Three stops. One at either end, the town hall square in the middle. North-east to south-west and back again. That's progress. Anyone who's against it isn't properly informed. Some things you have to listen to, others you don't. You can sit them out. After all, the town hall's not a dustbin. It's only the embittered who make a fuss. It's only the disqualified who complain. But of course you have to tell it like it is. It affects us. It affects the future. It affects everything. The holes in the road don't matter. Those we can accept. In winter, they freeze over as soon as they fill with water. Children can sail little boats in them in summer. That's nice. Everything has pros and cons. The olden days weren't better, just different. Everything changes. Everything flows.

Everything costs money. The holes in the budget are bigger than the holes in the road. The holes in the budget are bigger than the marshy holes on the outskirts of town. That sounds good. Did you get that? Just an idea. A suggestion. Politics doesn't get to dictate to the press. No one gets to dictate anything to anyone. There's far too much talk everywhere as it is. Untruthful talk. Improper talk. The school renovation is not on the agenda. Nothing is on the agenda. Nor is the business with the donations. Which isn't true, incidentally. Some things get exaggerated. A lot gets misrepresented. Everything, really. The truth is malleable, like hot iron. Reality is a matter of opinion. Anyone who wants to can inform themselves. Anyone who doesn't want to will be informed. That's freedom. Did you get that? Excellent. From the side, as well? A tram is one thing, the poison in Buxter's ground pork is something else entirely. You mustn't confuse them, lump them all together, measure them by the same yardstick. There's a time for everything. There's a place for everything. Where would we be otherwise? Hang on. Not like that. That's not right. Preposterous, and dangerous to boot. Corruption has no name. A name is what gives a person dignity. Do you see the priest lying in the road, his back like a burnt pastry? Did you hear about the dead boy they pulled out of the marsh yesterday? Have you read about the last will and testament of Karl Jonas, who wanted his grave filled with earth from his field? About the firefighters crawling over a mountain of rubble to search for the living and the dead? Think about it. Think what you like. Believe, as soon as you can permit yourself to do so. Belief is actually knowledge. Knowledge becomes opinion. Write that down!

The child with no name. The lost light. Buxter's last deed. A dead man in the field. Three dead beneath glass and stone. The mayor's dream in ruins. Silence in the town hall. Who does the town belong to? Whose is the woman's red shoe? A grave too many. The spiralling costs of road building. No resignations, but a lot of questions. Winter is here! No summer this year! Kobielski's celebrates its anniversary! It was murder! It was manslaughter! It was just a mistake. Attempt on the record in the town hall square. Public sector workers' strike – this is no joke! Graffiti of shame. Goodbye, Uncle Abu! A frosty spring. An autumn of decisions. The end of the tea dance? Resignation as early as this year? Paulstadt's big chance. The pride of Paulstadt. Paulstadt in shock! Paulstadt's most beautiful floral decorations. The decisive night. Baby joy in retirement home! Neighbours quarrel over plum tree.

My mother is dead.

My mother is dead. The house smelled of her for a long time afterwards. Her shadow flitted across the wallpaper in the hall, and there were noises everywhere. The rustling of paper in her drawer. The chink of a coffee cup. The tapping of her footsteps in the room, soft and quiet on the rug. The shadow disappeared and the noises diminished or altered over time. The creaking of floorboards and the crockery vibrating in the kitchen cupboard had nothing to do with her any more. I sit alone, listening into the dark.

It was for you that I kept going. But it wasn't the same. Back then, in the kitchen, I saw the letter in your lap, clasped between your hands. It was dirty with earth. You didn't smile. Yet I so wanted you to. I didn't want to hear anything. I wanted to fight for my childhood. I wanted to yell in your face: 'I am a child and I want to stay a child for ever. I want to stay your child!' I didn't yell. I did it for you. Was it enough? I don't know. I wish I'd looked at things more carefully. I wish I'd looked at things less carefully. I wish you could be proud of me. Don't be angry with me. I looked behind curtains. In the end, I pulled the final curtain aside and saw that, behind it, there was nothing. I wish I had nothing to regret. And that's the whole truth.

Martin Reynart

The rain was sudden and heavy. As if the water had been accumulating for half the summer and was now disgorging itself over the town in a single, monumental downpour. We sat in the car, drinking beer and listening to music. Tom in the back, Kath in the driver's seat, me beside her. It was her father's car and she'd only had her driving licence a few weeks. She said he'd kill her if she let anyone else behind the wheel. He'd tie her to the rear axle by her hair and drag her over the fields. That day she was wearing a short, knitted dress, and just two hours earlier I'd seen the fine hairs on her thighs shining in the evening sun. The sun had set some time ago and her legs had been swallowed by the darkness, and we sat there like ghosts, not yet drunk enough to feel really good, and it was Saturday evening and the road, the town, the whole world was dead, and the only thing moving was the rain, drumming on the bodywork and running in wide streaks down the windows.

'Hey, Kath, didn't I see you with that jerk the other day?' asked Tom. 'What's his name again?'

'The only jerk around here is you.'

'Forgotten his name. Great big guy. Arms like a monkey.'

'You're the jerk. And you're drunk.'

'I wish.'

'Leave her alone,' I said.

'What's it to you?' said Kath. 'Think I can't defend myself?'

'Dunno what I think.'

'We women are incapable of doing anything without you, is that it?'

'I never said that.'

'Do you two always have to ruin everything? It's Saturday night,' said Tom.

I'd have liked to punch him in the face, sitting back there with his face half in shadow and a beer wedged between his knees. It was always like this. He'd start it, I'd just join in, but I'd always get blamed for everything. We were supposed to be best friends, though, and I probably didn't want to destroy the myth. A gust of wind slapped the windscreen, and for a moment I had the feeling something heavy had fallen from the sky right onto our car, right here, in the deadest part of the deadest town in the world.

'Summer's over,' I said.

'We're almost out of beer,' said Tom.

'I've had enough,' said Kath.

We drove around for a bit. Westwards down the approach road out of town. No one followed us. No one came the other way. We were the only light, the only living thing for miles. The wind whipped the rain across the asphalt, and at the roadside the earth seemed to be boiling.

Something shot across the road in front of us, and there was a muffled thud. I was catapulted first forwards, then to the side; something hard slammed into my chest, maybe the steering wheel, maybe the gearstick, I don't know, and for a moment I couldn't breathe. Then I was sitting upright again. I was breathing, but it sounded weird, a hollow, dark bubbling, and I was in terrible pain. I looked around. The car was tilted forwards and the bonnet was buried in a field. The engine had cut out, but the headlights were still on. The radio was dangling from the dashboard on its wires, hissing. The windscreen had shattered, and it fractured the light into thousands of tiny jigsaw pieces. Something was dripping onto my hand, but it wasn't beer.

'What was that?' I heard Tom say in the back. He was sitting there just as he had been a few moments ago. But there was a long, gaping wound in his cheek, and blood was pouring out at the bottom and running down his chin.

'A fox or something,' I said. 'Not a person, anyway.'

'How do you know?'

'Too small. And there's no one around out here.'

'You sound weird.'

'I know.'

'What's that on your shirt? Is it blood?'

Kath, who'd been sitting slumped over with her face on her knees, sat up. 'He'll kill me!' she said. 'He'll kill me!'

'Oh, come on, they'll be able to fix it.'

'No,' she said. 'Just look at the radio!'

Suddenly the car interior lit up. A vehicle was rushing towards us; it slowed and stopped. A man came running through the rain. 'Are you OK?'

Tom rolled down the window. 'No,' he said. 'This guy's bleeding and making weird noises.'

'Only when I breathe,' I said.

'Oh God,' said the man, staring at us. 'Stay where you are. I'll get help!' He stumbled back to his car and drove off.

'He'll kill me,' said Kath. 'He'll kill us all.'

'I need some fresh air,' I said, and got out of the car.

'The steering wheel's broken, too,' I heard her wail.

It was pitch dark outside. It wasn't raining so hard any more, and I imagined that the cool air was doing me good. The earth squelched under my feet. With every step I sank up to my ankles in mud. When I was sure they couldn't see me any more, I fell to my knees and started to cry. It felt as if there was something stuck deep inside me, and there was.

I reached inside my shirt and tried to touch the spot, but it was just a wet, pulsating hole. I leaned forward and spat a cascade of blood. I laid my face on the ground and screamed into the mud. I thought of Kath and her father. He'd kill her. Or she him. I wouldn't put it past her. And then she'd run off with Tom and marry him and everything. Suddenly it all became clear. It was all just a game, and everyone was playing against me. They'd finished me off. Tom and Kath. The two of them. Him especially. He was scooping the lot. He was the victor.

He'd joined the class the year after me. When he stood at the front and quietly said his name, it was clear that our social hierarchy was about to change. You could see it in the girls' eyes: they were crazy about him. About his black hair that made him look a bit like an Indian. His long eyelashes. His smooth skin. And that damned soft, soapy voice. They put him in the seat next to me, and inevitably we became friends. But in our friendship we were on different levels. Perhaps it sounds stupid, but I sometimes felt like a whimpering puppy when I was around him. It was just how he made you feel.

When the weather was nice we'd all hang out in the park, or in the field at night. We'd drink beer and try the pills we'd nicked from our parents' medicine cabinets. We'd sort them by colour and shape and swallow them one after the other. Usually nothing happened, but sometimes they'd really knock you out. In my memory it's always spring. It's warm, there's beer and pills and swarms of those feathery white things floating through the air. We were both after Kath. Wherever she was, we were there too. Maybe the reverse was also true. No idea who was first in love with whom. We were all in love with life. I didn't think I was jealous, but one day I said to her she shouldn't throw herself at him like a whore. She just closed her eyes and held her face up to the sun. I think she told him, later.

The pain. It felt as if something was boring deeper and deeper into my chest with every move. So much blood. I think by now there was more coming from my mouth than from the hole in my chest. The bubbling had turned into a kind of hoarse snorting. I was an animal, and this was my voice. I crawled into the earth, tunnelled a hole for myself with my head. Then I was gone.

He kissed me once. We were at the field with Schwitters and the others, and I was lying on my back on the mayor's tombstone when he suddenly knelt over me and grinned. 'What are you doing, dickhead?' I asked, and the next thing I knew he'd pressed his great damp mouth onto mine. I'll smash his face in, I thought, I'll break something and keep on smashing him in the face until he stops moving. But I didn't. I didn't do anything; I just lay there with his tongue in my mouth and couldn't move. Then he got up and fetched a beer. I acted like it was all just a stupid joke, but I could have wept.

Voices. Calling, shouting. I raised my head and glanced back at the road. There were at least three or four cars standing there. In the blue light the ground appeared to be steaming. Police officers were all talking at the same time. I recognized two of them. A fireman rushed, crouching, from his vehicle to the damaged car and back again. Kath was standing by the ambulance, a blanket around her shoulders, talking to a man. Tom was inside, lying on the stretcher. I recognized him by his trainers. Blue with yellow soles. The two of them bathed in light. There are no angels. The light is there for everyone. It was still raining. But the strange thing was that the rain was falling very slowly. Silvery cords from the blackness, as if in slow motion. Someone called my name. I didn't move. What were they to me? I was an animal in the earth. Tom, said the rain on my face. Tom. Tom. Tom. Tom. Tom. His blue-and-yellow shoes were mine once. Everything he owned had once belonged to me. I don't need it any more. Their torches flicker through the darkness. The fox appears right in front of me. He stretches his front paws stiffly away from him, then lies down beside me with his muzzle against my face. Just stay there, don't move, he whispers. They won't find us.

Linda Aberius

I

I can't say why, but I'm quite sure: it's a mountain in the south. And right at the top there's a hotel. It's a bright, open building. There's a clear view on all sides. The cloud layer is spread out below us, infinitely white and wide. It's winter. We've been here a while already (a few days?), and I'm surrounded by good people. But not a single face . . .

I start to feel uneasy. A premonition of departure. I have the sense that I belong. But to whom? Suddenly he's standing beside me. We talk. The back of his neck and his hair smell good, and he's smiling. We sit, and I put my hands in my lap. The fabric is cool beneath my fingers. His explanations are friendly, but firm. He talks with his head bowed. I hear no words yet understand everything.

It's time. Most of them are already downstairs. And at this moment I realize that I'm alone again. It's very simple, someone calls over to me, he's gone up to the bedroom! With her! Those two are together now.

Later, I walk down the mountain path with quick, light steps. The cold wind is blowing in my face. Behind my eyes, though, it's hot. They're up at the top, far behind me.

I love you . . .

A thing is lying by the roadside. Its face is covered in dust and its eyes look like blue puddles in limestone. Suddenly I feel terrible pain, and that's when I notice that my left arm is missing. It's been torn off at the shoulder. Horrified, I start to run down the mountain. I close my eyes. The pain slowly subsides, and finally, finally . . .

II

A rumbling issues from the heart of the night. Cold stars snow from the sky. The child lies deep in the forest. Don't bother, I say, you won't find it . . . I feel a degree of *schaden-freude*. I press my face into the warmth, because I know that now it's all right. Now nothing else can happen. Gradually, silence falls. Not a breath of wind. I hibernate in your armpit.

III

Everything here is filthy, the man says, gesticulating wildly; a filthy, stinking mess, but at least it's fun! I walk up Markt-strasse. The shops line up in a row on either side like brightly painted boxes. You feel like just muddling them all together. What are you, Paulstadt? Your roots scarcely go deeper than the town hall basement. The rats are gnawing already! someone shouts, staggering across the pavement. He's the personification of stupidity. I know this, but I can't do anything about it. The man laughs. His arms are flags of farewell. The smell of burnt wood drifts towards me from the church square. And that's when I realize: it's just a dream within a dream. There will be no awakening.

Bernard Silbermann

I can hear them. I hear their footsteps on the small, round pebbles of the path. I recognize them by their footsteps. I know who they are long before they stand above me and start talking.

I know what they're saying before they open their mouths.

I hear them when they're silent, too. I know them.

Their footsteps.

Pom. Pom. Pom. Soft and heavy. Pom. Pom. Pom. Slowly, slowly; everything takes time.

Right, Camille?

Good morning, Bernard. It's a nice morning today. Warm. You should smell the earth. It smells of autumn. Aromatic. And kind of smoky, somehow.

I can smell the earth, Camille, how could I not? My skull is packed with it. But it doesn't smell smoky down here. It just smells of earth, sometimes damp, sometimes less so.

Maybe it's just the air. I think someone's burning dead leaves over by the south-west entrance. They always do that at this time of year. What does death smell like, Bernard?

Death smells of salt. Have you brought flowers? You know I don't like flowers. I do appreciate it, though. Did you buy them from Gregorina? Is her shop still there? No, you stole them, didn't you? You sneaked into the park before sunrise. Regnier will find the cut stems later and make something daft out of them. Put them down. Stroke your fingers over the petals again. It'll make you feel good. You're a thief, Camille!

It's strange, but as soon as you enter the cemetery the weather changes. There's hardly any wind here, and when it's cloudy it all still seems bright and spacious. Even when it rains it's nicer than in town. The rain falls silently and is swallowed by the earth. It's very quiet where you are.

I've long since forgotten what the sky looks like. And it isn't quiet where we are. On the contrary: it's full of sounds and voices. There is scratching and gnawing and scraping. And it's not just creatures. Even the roots are noisy. Sometimes there's a rumbling, too. The rumbling comes from deep down and slowly swells. You want to curl up and escape it but there's nothing left to curl, and then it dies away again. There is no silence. Anywhere.

The Field

Will you look at that: the weeds are already eating through your tombstone. And it wasn't what you'd call cheap. It'll last a few generations, the stonemason told us, do you remember? He had to shout because he didn't bother turning off the grinder.

He was a crook. Bellowed the whole time, and his face was streaked with marble dust. Crooks and criminals, the lot of them. They bare their gold teeth and wipe their car bonnets and door handles and tombstones with little dust cloths and talk to you about quality and status, and already you've fallen into their trap. What are you doing? Stop scraping at the crack. There's no point, you'll only break your fingernails. Are they still red, Camille? Are your fingernails still red?

There was one that was even nicer. And more expensive! It had fine reddish veins, and if you placed your hand on it, it was warm, like wood. From Italy. Or Chile? Yes, it was from Chile, a real South American, the stonemason said. Perhaps we should have picked that one.

Leave it, Camille. Do you really think you can do anything about it? It's just weeds. Weeds and moss. What's the matter, Camille?

I'm sad.

That stuff is more enduring than any stone, no matter where it comes from or how much it costs. He cheated us, that's how it is. They cheated all of us . . .

Do you know, for years after you died I kept finding your hairs? You hardly had any left when I met you, but the apartment was full of them nonetheless. I found the last hair a year ago. It was definitely yours. Short and blonde, almost white.

It's nice to hear you, Camille.

Shall I tell you a story? It's pretty gruesome. But I think it's kind of funny, too. It's about Kobielski. You know he's got this thing about lawnmowers. He's crazy about them; I think he's got more in his garage than he has cars in his showroom. Then up and down the garden every Sunday! A godawful racket, like a motor race, and the stink of petrol to boot, do you remember? He was at it again recently. We were sitting on the patio, warm day, sun shining, and then it kicks off: Kobielski in Speedos and sandals, white belly, white legs, pushing his latest acquisition back and forth across the lawn, massive thing with an engine like a tractor. This goes on for about an hour. At least. It's noisy, it stinks, Kobielski's having fun, the usual. And then it happens. I don't know why; maybe he slipped in his ratty sandals, maybe the blades hit a stone or a root – anyway, he suddenly wrenches the lawnmower into the air, staggers backwards and drops it on the ground with a crash. There's a horrible noise and then it all goes quiet.

Who do you mean by 'we'?

You all right, Kobielski? I ask. But he just stands there, staring at us over the garden fence, and doesn't say a word. I notice he's sweating profusely. The sweat is streaming down his face and shoulders. You all right? I ask again, and now he shakes his head. No, he says, I don't think so. He lifts the lawnmower slightly and his foot appears underneath. Where the big toe was, there's a dark hole with blood seeping out of it. The rest of the foot doesn't seem to be damaged. As far as I can tell, even the sandal is still in one piece. Kobielski looks down at the grass. Then he bends over and picks something up. From a distance it looks like a round white mushroom. But it's his toe. He holds it up and says: Maybe they can put it back on. He says it quite calmly, but his face is white as a sheet.

Who's 'we', Camille? Who's sitting on the patio with you on a Sunday afternoon?

Anyway, they didn't manage to put the toe back on. Kobielski told us he keeps it in a preserving jar in his kitchen cupboard, right next to the spice box. But I'm not sure I believe him, you know what he's like.

Yes.

I'm going away, Bernard.

Why . . . what are you saying? Of course I know what he's like. He's a nutter. He's just . . . Kobielski. What can I say?

I'm going to leave.

A preserving jar? That doesn't sound right to me. Nobody does a thing like that. Does he still feed the birds? He must have realized by now that he's killing them. The sugar and the fat kill them. The birds die of high blood pressure. Or they burst. The bread swells up in their stomachs until they burst. The bushes are riddled with exploded bird carcasses. And then the foxes come from the fields, or worse, the rats from the canal. That's probably why he does it. He's a nutter, that Kobielski, I think all that petrol has clouded his brain . . .

Bernard . . .

Tell me what's the matter, Camille? Your voice sounds hard. And don't keep calling me Bernard. It sounds so serious. The first time you called me that, I knew there was no going back. I stood there and I suddenly felt like a man. That was good, but something was lost, too. In every moment, something is lost. Do you remember what you always used to call me? Call me that again. I'd like us to call each other by our old names again, Camille.

I won't miss Paulstadt. It never meant anything to me, you know that. But I will think about the time we spent together. It was a good time, and I'm grateful to you for it, Bernard. I've had a lot to do these last few weeks, but it's all sorted now. And with the money from the house, I'll be fine. It was really quick. Two signatures, that was all.

You've sold our house.

A lorry for the furniture. Yesterday I picked cherries again. A whole basketful, dark red, almost black. We'll have a garden again, but no cherry tree. I'll be able to see the mountains, though. Do you remember how much I missed the mountains? Soon I'll be able to see them when I wake up just by looking out of the window, isn't that lovely? And someone's going to come. Someone will take care of you, Bernard. Of the plants. And the weeds. They're supposed to scrape the moss out of the cracks and seal the marble once a month. And sand down and polish the slab again. I want it to reflect the moon.

Stop crying, Camille.

The flowers are really pretty. I think you'd like them.

The house. How much did you get for it? What about our wardrobe? It's older than the house. You can't just take it with you. It wouldn't survive the journey. Unless you took it apart. But the wood has gone brittle with age. And who would glue it back together? Don't you remember us standing in front of it? We imagined the grain was a map with roads and paths, all of which we'd travel down some day. And you laughed, Camille. Don't you remember? You couldn't stop laughing!

Goodbye, Bernard.

And don't try to get it down the stairs in one piece. It's too heavy, it'd fall apart. It's not the stuff we kept in it that counts. That doesn't matter. What was it, anyway? Tools. Old bedlinen. Christmas decorations, things like that. It's the wardrobe that counts. And your laugh. Your laugh, Camille, don't you understand?

Camille?

Kurt Kobielski

The night before, I'd let myself be persuaded and took a '67 Transit on sale or return. It had character, and we spent the whole morning scratching big black chunks of rust out of the oil tank. There were some bits that needed welding, too. By midday I'd had enough. I went to the park and sat on a bench. It was cool in the shade of the chestnut trees. High above, two planes flew over and drew a frayed cross in the sky.

We should fit it with a new rear axle, I thought, that at least.

A bird came hopping over. It sat in front of me for a while and didn't do anything. Then it flew off. I leaned back and stretched out my legs. My trousers were covered in oil and there were holes in the knees. Viewed from above, my knees looked like little white faces.

I couldn't help grinning.

A woman walked past in jeans. The jeans were tight, and

her bum quivered or swayed or shimmied, while over on the grass a dog was running backwards and forwards. His tongue flapped alongside his mouth, like a pink sleeve I once saw dangling out of the window of a school bus.

I was tired, but in an agreeable sort of way. Nothing hurt, and I wasn't hungry or thirsty.

Maybe I could keep the Transit, I thought.

There was a rustling in the tree above me, and immediately afterwards a little white blob of shit landed right beside me on the bench. Splat! it went, and in that moment I realized: today will have been the happiest day of your life.

And it was.

Connie Busse

The sun on the window. That's where it starts. I should have cleaned it, I think, should have given all the windows another thorough clean before we set off. Too late now. The windows are like magnets for dust. God knows how it manages to stick to that smooth glass surface. And leave streaks. It always leaves these streaks.

Fred's hairy leg rubs against mine. He knows how this works. Not too hard, but not too soft, either. Definitely not too soft. No arousal so early in the morning. It's only through this non-arousal that arousal might in fact be possible. That's the unspoken agreement. He places the sole of his foot over my cold toes like a heat pack. He gives me an innocent look, face half-hidden under the covers, and moves his chin rhythmically. He looks like a puppy. The scratching of beard on fabric is our morning music. He says: I'd like to bury myself in you. I say: I should have cleaned the windows. He presses himself against me and whispers in my ear: There are other things we could do.

Then Maya and the dog come running in. She's naked; her nightdress has got lost somewhere between here and the bathroom. She stops, looks at us, doesn't understand, doesn't want to. Sunspots quiver in her hair. Finally she laughs and throws herself onto the bed with us. Are we going today? Yes! Really today? Yes! The dog jumps up and down at the end of the bed, barking like mad.

Maya's ear, very close.

The little hairs behind it, exquisitely fine.

Her cheek. Her small, round shoulder.

Her laughter. Our laughter. The dog barking.

Fred huffing and growling, great big dangerous creature of the blanket cave.

The car, of course, is packed to the rafters. As if we were moving, not going on holiday. We are, says Fred; we're moving to another routine. And he packs a big box of books. He's read them all. Several times, most of them. One he even wrote. It's a sort of chronicle of his home town, entitled *Paulstadt: A Town Without a Neighbourhood*. He only wrote it so he could carry it around with him all the time and use it when necessary to justify his work as parish librarian. He needs familiar things around him, he says, foreign countries are quite unfamiliar enough. But now he's checking the oil. And the water. The tyre pressure, too. He does this by clumsily groping the sides of the tyres with his fingers. It's a serious business. I used to love him for efforts like these. Maya is whining. Her beach ball needs blowing up. It can only come if it's blown up, otherwise you can't see the dolphin's face, and we can't leave without it. Fred blows it up. His freshly shaven cheeks are pink and shiny. Maya is happy. Ready? Ready. Blanket, child and dog on the back seat. Here we go. In we get. Driving away. Maya and the blue-and-yellow dolphin laugh out of the rear window. Is Paulstadt disappearing, Mama? Yes, my love, like everything in this world.

Fields. Dark, thin trees in the distance.

Fred's hands on the steering wheel. His fingers tapping in time to 'Let's Get It On'.

A truck full of pigs. Their ears and snouts between the wooden slats.

My face in the windowpane at the border station.

The official's lazy wave.

The yellow landscape. Lemons. Olives. Half-finished buildings. And, by the side of the road, an actual donkey.

Little sounds from Maya in her sleep.

My hand on the open window.

*

Our holiday home sits slightly above the small coastal town with a view across the harbour out to sea. There used to be a fishing industry, now there's just folklore. Some restaurants and tourist bars, half a dozen souvenir shops, the little beach, and right behind it the ten-storey hotel with dancing at the poolside bar in the evening. Fred loves it here. He says it's not ugly enough to be off-putting, but not beautiful enough to get unnecessarily excited about. Strangely, I think he's right. Nothing is too much here, almost everything is just enough. There's something soothing about this; also, we can afford it. This is the fourth time we've come, and Maya recognizes 'her' things again. The room with the blue bed. The bucket and spade in the garage. The mouldy patch on the kitchen ceiling that's always changing shape; this year it looks like the profile of an angry man in a hat. In the morning we go swimming, in the afternoon we sit on the terrace, and in the evening we eat in the only authentic fish restaurant on the harbour promenade. Umberto, our landlord, tells us the fish comes deep-frozen from Norway, which is why it tastes so good. We're OK with that. The harbour air is Italian, at least, and probably the vegetables as well.

We lie on the beach and watch Maya digging. She squats in a hole right up to her shoulders and digs deeper and deeper, serious, concentrating hard. Look, that's our child, says Fred. Yes, I say, I don't think she's the brightest spark. True, says

Fred, but she's turned out pretty well otherwise. We both nod. I try to smile. It's unbearably hot. I'm sweating under the suntan oil. There should really be a breeze coming off the sea. Two tourist boats are rocking far out on the water. But there's no wind, nothing's moving, and the sand is sticking to my forehead. I don't like sand. It gets stuck on your forehead and in your armpits and between your toes and it chafes the skin. I read once that there are more bacteria on the surface of a grain of sand than there are people in the average small town. Fred says that's nonsense, but secretly he thinks the same. It's in moments like this that we understand each other. Now Maya wants an ice cream. You've already had two, I say. She immediately starts crying and lets herself fall over. She just pitches forward and cries furiously into the sand. That's it for today, then, I say. No way! says Fred. He jumps up, grabs our daughter, who's already laughing again, drapes her across his shoulders and runs into the water with her. I put my sunhat over my face and hear them spluttering and shouting. Now that my mouth is hidden, I too make sounds. A gentle clicking of the tongue, a humming and murmuring underneath the sun-warmed straw.

Climbing over a lump of concrete on the way back from the beach, I slip and cut my wrist on a piece of metal. The wound isn't deep, and it's two centimetres long at most, but for some reason I'm unusually upset by the sight of the broken skin, and I squat there staring at the blood as it drips onto the rock between my feet. It's not so bad, says Fred cheerfully; we'll put a bandage on it, it'll be fine. But the stupid thing was rusty, I say. Come on, you're a big girl now, he says, and laughs like a fifteen-year-old.

The days pass. A relaxation sets in that is really just increasing lethargy. It's too hot to go for a walk, open a book, or at least have sex. Even thoughts seem to evaporate in the heat. A static blanket of cloud has been hanging over the sea for days now. It's grey, and turns yellowish red towards evening. It's pretty, but Maya says the sky is sick with a fever. At least she's happy. She likes everything, can laugh at everything. At the sick sky. At the funny sea. At the clouded fish eyes on her plate. At the pink snake of strawberry ice cream crawling across the back of her hand. At Fred's contortions in the water. Since I had my fall, Fred and Maya have been going to the beach without me. The wound has got infected; my wrist is in a bandage and I don't want it to come into contact with sand and dirt and salt water. Fred changes the bandage every morning, and afterwards Maya draws a little face on it. It's smiling, to comfort me. And it does. I spend the mornings on the bed with the window open. I enjoy being alone. The dog doesn't count. He lies in the doorway, asleep mostly, his tongue hanging out of his mouth like a rag.

*

The dog's panting.

The quiet squeak of the ceiling fan.

There's no murmur from the sea. The murmur comes from the road on the other side of the hill.

The murmur.

The squeak.

The panting.

The white sky.

The white room.

They burst in, smelling of the sea. Fred tears off his T-shirt and does press-ups on the floor. With each one his belly slaps on the tiles. His back is bright red, and sand trickles from his hair. He crawls towards the bed, then back towards the door, making gurgling, bubbling sounds. He doesn't see the little puddle left by the dog's tongue. He's a crab now. So is Maya. We're crabs, and we've brought you the sea, she shouts, pouring a bucketful of wet shells and pebbles onto the sheet. I pretend to be pleased. Haha, I shout, haha!

I'm woken in the night by the creaking and slapping of the fishing boats in the harbour. The wind has picked up, presaging bad weather. Fred is breathing deeply and quietly. His mouth is half open. He looks like before. I creep into Maya's room, lean over her bed and look at her face. It's so beautiful

I could cry. I don't know why everything I do quietly always feels like farewell.

Only two more days until we go home. The storm was bad. The force of the waves pushed one of the tourist boats up against the quay wall and ripped a big hole in the wood. Umberto says there's nothing to be done about it, but it's their own fault: the boat's at least fifty years old and held together by nothing but paint and the owner's prayers. Fuel for the bonfire at the harbour festival. Maia cries. She sobs uncontrollably in my arms and can't explain why. Later she says she's sad about the harbour festival, that we won't be here to see it. And she feels sorry for the boat. The hole looks as if it was made by an underwater creature. It's sure to die now. In the bathroom I take off her blouse and press my face against the damp patch of her tears.

On our last day, Fred and I sit on the terrace looking out at the sea. Maya's asleep in our bed. About twenty minutes ago I put on a blissful smile especially for Fred. It's intended to signal my fundamental approval of him, of the holiday we've just had, of life in general. Smiling fixedly, I gaze into the distance and say: Here, beside the sea, I'm always aware of how badly I need freedom. Infinity, with all its possibilities, of closeness and distance. Fred says: Aha. I say: It really is paradise. Fred says: Yes, but it stinks a bit after the storm, I think it's the seaweed drifting in the water over there. I take a sip of my orange juice, then I put my hand on his forearm and say: You can't admit that it's paradise because you're afraid of being driven out. Your fear of being driven out is so great that you have to drive out the idea of paradise before it can even occur to you. That's possible, he says. I take back my hand and have another sip of juice. Gulls scream above our heads. He says: The seaweed spreads on the surface of the water. It forms a thick, slimy carpet that rots in the sun and suffocates all life underneath. I look at him and say: You're a nincompoop. No one says that, my pet, says Fred, that's a Fifties word; you'll only come across it in trashy novels or kitschy TV soaps these days. What else can I call you, I ask. Don't know, says Fred, idiot? If Maya wasn't sleeping in our bed, we could go and lie down in it now, I say. He looks at me sideways and says: I love you. I hate that. It forces you to respond. It's impossible not to respond to *I love you*. I take another swig of orange juice. It tastes unusually sweet and good. I slowly drain the glass and put it down. Then I say: I love you, too.

Just then, Umberto comes around the corner. His face is red and damp, as if he's got a fever. Come, please, he says, I think something has happened. We follow him around the house. I glance at Maya through the window. She's sleeping, with the dolphin-faced ball lying in bed beside her. Come, says Umberto. We walk a few hundred metres along the

road that winds up the heat-scorched hill. Look there, says
Umberto. Our dog is lying dead by the side of the road.
His coat is dishevelled and dirty. There's a gaping wound in
his belly, and something like a bluish, shimmering bubble
spilling out of it. Flies are buzzing around. Fred groans. It's
a sound I first heard him make a very long time ago. He
raises both hands, as if about to greet someone, then drops
them again, runs to the dog and falls on his knees beside
him. Umberto says: It was a car, the bends are tight. Yes, I
say, a car. He says: I'm sorry. I nod. Fred pushes his arms
under the body and tries to move it. He strokes the dog's
hair, just behind its ears, and waves his hands to chase away
the flies. It's strange; now, of all moments, I find myself
thinking of the first time we caught sight of each other.
He was standing outside the stationer's on Marktstrasse
with a piece of cake in his hand. I saw his face mirrored in
the shop window, and I saw a few cake crumbs fall to the
ground. He wasn't good-looking or otherwise remarkable,
but something about him touched me. I think I felt sorry
for him.

Maya appears behind us. She stands in the road, barefoot,
in her swimming costume, her hands shielding her eyes from
the sun. Mama? she says, Mama? Get inside the house, says
Fred. For Christ's sake, take our child and get her inside the
house!

*

I imagine:

    The two men up the hill.

    Panting.

    Their silent solemnity.

    Their hands.

    The sweat on Fred's forehead, on his neck.

    The soft sound of clods of earth falling on the dead body.

We leave that evening. Umberto gives us two bottles of wine as a parting gift. He picks Maya up and says: You'll be too heavy for me next year. She throws her head back and stares at the bedroom ceiling. Fred sits behind the wheel; he's determined to drive the whole way. We wave as we set off. Umberto shouts something unintelligible, then he's gone. The night is warm. The sky is cloudy. Hardly any stars. The moon, from time to time. The roads are quiet, there's little traffic. It'll be all right, says Fred. Sure, I say. Everything in here smells of him, he says. Yes, I say, we should get the car cleaned, Kobielski's offering a deep clean now. What's that supposed to be, asks Fred, a deep clean? They do everything, I say, from the exhaust pipe to the floor mats. They even brush the crumbs out of the glove compartment. What crumbs, asks Fred. I don't know, I say, crumbs or whatever. Fred turns on the car radio. How often have we heard this song, he asks. No idea, I say, have we ever heard it? He turns it off again. I open the window. The air seems completely filled with the chirping of crickets. Close it, Maya's sleeping, says Fred. I close the window and clamp my hand between my thighs. The cut is hurting under the bandage. The pain is hot and throbbing. I close my eyes and lean my head back. Half-asleep, I think: you deserve this, this is your punishment. But for what? I wake and see the lights of the night slip by. We drive on without speaking. Then suddenly Fred says: She didn't ask a single question, do you realize that? She's a child, I say. Since when do children not ask questions, he says, I mean, her dog was run over. Perhaps she knows there are no answers, I say; and besides, it was our dog. Sometimes you're a bit too smart for me, he says, I can't keep up. I say: Stop it.

Maya wakes with the sunrise. How much further? We'll soon be there, darling. See those trees over there, they're poplars, not cypresses. Poplars are the guardians of the fields. They watch over our potatoes. And the tomatoes? And the tomatoes, those especially.

I unwrap the bandage around my wrist. Leave it, says Fred, we'll go to a doctor when we get home. The wound is dark and wet, the skin at the edges inflamed. I open the window and hold my arm into the wind. What's that line, Mama? What do you mean, darling? The red line on your arm, look, it looks like a road. Yes, darling, you're right, it's a thin red road.

The skyline of Paulstadt materializes in front of us

through the morning mist. Fred slaps both hands on the wheel and shouts: You see, you were wrong, it didn't disappear, it's still here!

Yes, shouts Maya, it's still here! It's still here!

The first surge of commuters comes towards us on the approach road. Maya waves. No one waves back. It's going to be a good day, says Fred, summer's not over yet, not by a long chalk. I see a movement across the fields, like a fleeting shadow. And no clouds. No birds. Nothing but the big, big sky. I think I'd like to go straight to the doctor, I say, it might be best. Fred looks at me. Then he shifts down a gear and puts his foot on the accelerator. After that it all goes very fast.

Harry Stevens

A living person thinking about death. A dead person talking about life. What's the point? Neither side understands the other. There are intimations. And there are memories. Both can be deceptive.

Do you remember Richard Regnier? The one they called the madman. Maybe he was a bit mad, but then so was I, and that's what was good about it. That's what I thought, anyway, and what I still think, if this can be called thinking. We weren't exactly what you'd call friends. We didn't tell each other our secrets or anything like that. We just liked to spend time together, that's all there was to it.

One evening we'd arranged to meet in the town hall square. We were going to the Golden Moon for a beer or two. He was wearing his overalls and his filthy work boots. 'Hey, Regnier,' I said. 'I'm paying today.'

'Yes,' he said, 'you do that.'

We walked slowly, taking a couple of detours. It was one

of the last warm autumn evenings. The sky had clouded over. The air was damp and mild. Regnier took two apples from a pocket in his overalls. We ate them as we walked, and I have no idea why those two apples on that particular evening tasted so good to us.

The door of the Moon was open, the sour smell of spilt beer escaping from inside. Two men were sitting at the bar. One of them suddenly guffawed with laughter, then lowered his head and sat motionless.

'Come on,' said Regnier. 'Let's keep walking.'

We did a couple of circuits around Marktstrasse, then walked past the school and on towards the outskirts of town. Every few metres Regnier would pluck something from a bush or hedge, pop it in his mouth and chew it.

'What's that?' I asked.

'Greens,' he said. 'You wouldn't believe all the stuff that grows here right under your nose.'

By now, night had fallen. There were hardly any lights left in the windows. The moon was high above the trees. We left the last of the gardens behind us and walked along a path across the fields. Out here there was a gentle breeze, blowing the smell of fertilizer towards us. We walked for some time without saying a word. Suddenly Regnier stood still.

'I'd like to show you something,' he said.

'What?'

'The moon has to go in first.' He turned and pointed at the grey wall of cloud rising up above the town.

'Looks like it's going to rain,' I said.

'With any luck,' he said, and took a packet of cigarettes from his pocket.

'How long have you been a smoker?' I asked him.

'Don't know,' he said. 'Always.'

We lit our cigarettes. The match flared between our faces, and for a moment I felt as if I were beside a campfire. Two boys, somewhere out in the wilderness. We smoked and watched the clouds slowly drift in front of the moon.

'You like her, don't you?' Regnier asked suddenly.

'Who?'

'Oh, come on . . .'

'I've no idea,' I said. 'We've never said more than a few words to each other.'

'You like her,' he repeated.

I shrugged. 'You should look at her hands sometime. They're so slender and white.'

'Not the fingernails. They're dark around the edges, from the soil in the flowerpots.'

'Yes. So now what?'

'I don't know. I don't know how these things work. I like her. You like her. There's nothing more to be said.'

'No,' I said. 'Probably not.'

Darkness descended over the fields. It was as if night were falling only now.

'Here we go,' said Regnier.

He pointed in the direction of the Paulstadt leisure centre. Barely discernible, its outline rose up out of the flat fields in the distance.

'I don't see anything,' I said.

'Wait,' he said.

I stared into the darkness. I heard Regnier shift his weight from one foot to the other, the earth crunching beneath his feet, and I thought of her hands, the dark edges of her fingernails.

'Now,' he said.

At first there was nothing to be seen, just a black hill in the black night. But then I saw a light flicker along the lower edge. It was a soft, floating light, and it suddenly seemed to lengthen, describing a shimmering arc in the darkness. At the same moment the hill beneath began to glow. It glowed a delicate, almost translucent blue that swelled and ebbed, like a wave illuminated by the moon. Or like the back of an enormous, breathing beetle. It was a miracle, right there in front of us in the dark. It lasted a few seconds and then it was gone, the glow extinguished.

'It's the motorway slip road,' said Regnier. 'It's good around this time of the evening. There's hardly any traffic. Even four headlamps are too bright. And the sky has to be cloudy. But no rain, or it's too dark. When it's like this, it's just right.'

We waited and watched another three cars, then turned and headed home.

'We should get out of here someday,' I said.

'Yes,' said Regnier. 'We should do that.'

We said goodbye under the old tree on Kernerplatz. I stood for a while and watched him go, then I left in the opposite direction. I strolled down side streets and along the old cemetery wall towards Marktstrasse. The wind had picked up and was whispering in the tops of the trees. I was tired, but remembering what I had seen out in the fields made me feel light and free. The first fat drops began to fall as I turned onto Marktstrasse, and by the time I reached Sophie Breyer's tobacconist's it was bucketing down. For a moment, I imagined what it would be like just to stand there in the rain with my face upturned towards the sky. But then I started running, sprinting, because the street was deserted and I wanted to hear my feet splashing in the puddles.

As far as Regnier is concerned: one day he suddenly disappeared. No one in Paulstadt knew where he'd got to. He hadn't said goodbye to anyone, and no one saw him leave. He was just gone. I often thought of him. I tried in vain to imagine what sort of person he really was.

Years passed, and I grew old and died. At my funeral the

elderflower was in bloom, and a surprising number of people came. Regnier wasn't among them. He didn't come because he went before me, and I've never forgiven him for that.

Is my bench still there? And the birch tree?